KASH AND KARS

By STEVEN J. REPERGEL

For the love of family and great friendships.

Acknowledgments

Editors: Angelo Noal and Rachel Pieters

Proofreaders: Cyrus Gordon and Carolyn Delorme

Book Cover Design by Kristyn McQuiggan

Inside Illustrations by Jacquelyn Repergel

Chapter 1

A late-night drizzle covered downtown Los Angeles. On a street corner, an old movie theater flashed its colored lights around a marquee—"24-Hour Car Movie Marathon!"

Across the boulevard, the Toska restaurant, set in a late 19th century building, had an Open sign flickering through a window.

The sidewalks were nearly empty, except for one man moving briskly. His cowboy boots echoed off the wet concrete as the rain trickled from the brim of his felt fedora down to his weathered bomber. While eying the theater's headliners—*Le Mans, Bullitt, White Lightning,* and *The Last American Hero*—he walked up the front steps of the eatery and stepped inside.

He glanced around the low-lit room as classical music played through speakers embedded in the ceiling. It reminded him of a funeral parlor. Teal drapes, gray carpet, and gold wallpaper were certainly not to his taste. He approached the host, a small-statured man with a thin mustache, standing behind a podium.

"May I help you, sir?" the host asked.

"I'm looking for Dugan O'Sullivan."

"And you are?"

"Kash. Thomas Kash," he said, thinking his name might carry some clout, but it didn't even generate a brow lift.

Looking momentarily past the greeter and into a mirror, he removed his hat and checked his salt and pepper hair before unzipping his coat.

The greeter ran his finger down the reservation list as two large henchmen, standing at the back of the room near a booth, waved Kash over.

"Nevermind," he said, taking off his hat.

"Sir!" the host replied, before considering the consequences of trying to stop a man double his size. He backed off as Kash sauntered past.

Slipping between two stone-faced Russian heavies—who were even taller and bulkier than he was and with long, black ponytails that reached their waistlines—Kash appeared physically lacking by comparison. "Gentlemen," he said, acknowledging all the players.

Dugan sat behind a crescent-shaped table, outfitted like a gangster in an Italian suit with a white shirt and purple tie. He wore prescription-tinted glasses, had coarse gray hair, and a scowl that made it clear he was far from happy. A shiny, black cane and satchel lay next to him while he worked on devouring a filet mignon, served rare. Blood pooled out of the meat, saturating his potato and vegetables. "Glad you could make it on such short notice." He took another bite of steak and a mouthful of red wine. "I think you know the Mishka brothers, Abe and Jonah."

"Only by reputation," Kash replied. "And I know you never go anywhere without them."

"Sit down, will you?"

"No thanks, Dugan."

"Want a glass?" He held up a bottle labeled *Domaine Leroy Richebourg Grand Cru, 1949.* "Six grand it cost me. Can you believe it? They should use the money to update the place." He shook his head in dismay. "But the food's always good."

"I'm not staying long."

"What's your hurry?" Taking another sip, he slid his plate aside and dabbed his mouth with a white cotton napkin.

"I'm headed to the theater."

"Hah, you never could get your priorities in order," Dugan chortled, reaching into his case and pulling out a thick document. He tossed it on the table. It landed with a thud, rattling the silverware.

"What's this?"

"One helluva a deal, and a chance to avoid disaster."

"I only have two more payments," Kash said.

"Yes, but can you *really* come up with all of it?" He sipped his wine, savoring the flavor.

"What are you saying?"

"Until now, you've managed to scrounge up enough to make your typical repayments with interest."

"A lot of interest," Kash said.

"Yes, but that is the cost of doing business with me. Word on the street is that your sales are, how shall I put it? Lackluster."

A waiter stepped forward, menu in hand.

"Not for me, thank you," Kash said.

Dugan waved him off as he leaned back in the vinyl houndstooth seat, intertwined his fingers, and tapped his thumbs together.

"We've had a few setbacks, but nothing to be alarmed about."

"I don't get alarmed," he sneered. "I don't have to come up with the money. You do."

"You'll be paid like always, in full and on time." Kash felt his stomach twist as his optimism wavered.

"I know it wasn't easy for you to come crawling to me for a loan to start your operation," Dugan said. "But, since banks don't lend large amounts of money to ex-cons, your options were limited. And still are." He slid the document across the table.

"I'm not interested," Kash replied, clenching his fists.

"But you haven't even seen my offer."

"I don't need to."

Dugan slammed a hand down hard, nearly knocking over his wine. "Damn it! I'm not going to ask again." Starting to cough, he reached for his napkin and covered his mouth.

Abe rocked his head from side to side, loosening his neck muscles, while Jonah cracked his knuckles.

Rolling his eyes at their childish intimidation tactics, Kash picked up the papers and glanced through them, momentarily intrigued by the hundred pages of legal documents. "How much you offering?"

Regaining his composure, Dugan tossed the serviette aside. "For the whole thing, lock, stock, and barrel…" He had a crooked smile that exposed a mouth full of bad teeth. "…three million."

"That's it?" He sat the proposal in front of Dugan, then slid his hands into his coat pockets. "I was expecting three times that much."

"If your business was lucrative, perhaps. But from where I'm sitting, you're not even breaking even." He began to butter a roll. "What I'm offering would pay back the loan and provide a few extra dollars to help you move on. Of course, you could always come back and work for me, if you like."

"No thanks."

"This is a chance for you to wipe your hands clean of the whole thing." He pushed the document towards Kash.

"I understand that, but this is my dream. And besides, Donnie would never go for it."

"Trust me. It won't be too difficult to sell your business partner on the idea once he sees three million in cash. God knows he'd sell his mother for spare change." Another cough ensued.

"You should get that looked at. Could be pneumonia."

Dugan gulped the high-priced wine and cleared his throat. "I'm fine," he said hoarsely.

Out of the kitchen, a young server swung by with a special delivery. "Excuse me, gentlemen." He carefully maneuvered his way to the table. "Your shark fin soup, sir."

"Ah, finally." Dugan's eyes brightened as the bowl was set before him. Steam rose up to his flared nostrils as he inhaled. He gave a quick nod, sending the waiter scurrying away.

"Why do you want my company anyway? You running out of places to launder your money?"

He responded with a careless shrug and picked up a spoon. "What does it matter? All I want from you is an answer. Yes or no. It's that simple."

"You make it easy. The answer's no. Three million dollars just ain't enough."

Dugan scowled, flung down his utensils, and struggled to his feet. The brothers instantly moved in to help.

"I can do it!" he barked, refusing assistance. "Your business is like anything else. It's worth nothing until somebody buys it." He took the serrated knife from his plate, blood dripping from the blade, and used it as a pointer, coming close enough to stick Kash in the chest.

"Easy, Dugan. This is my favorite coat."

Dugan's hand was shaking, his face pale and sickly. He took the sharp end of the knife and jammed it into the tabletop.

"I also have my crew to think about."

Erupting with laughter, Dugan nearly lost his footing. "Stop, you're killin' me! You worried about those old cons?" He clapped his hands, thoroughly amused. "That's a good one."

"*Ex*-cons," Kash noted, unamused. "And, I'm giving them a chance to make good."

"You couldn't be any more off the mark!" Dugan tapped his cane on the floor like a judge summoning order to his court. "They're a bunch of hoodlums, vagabonds, a skid mark on the underwear of society." He began to perspire heavily. He reached for a handkerchief in his coat pocket and dabbed his face. "Why I'm surprised they haven't robbed you blind and left you for dead."

"They've always had my back."

"For now, maybe, but it's only a matter of time before they burn down your operation with you in it. Just you wait."

"Sorry, Dugan. My company is not for sale." Kash glanced at his watch. "Now if you'll excuse me, I have a show to catch."

"Just remember one thing." Dugan sat down to finish his meal. "When you default on your loan, and you will, I'll take full control of your company, and you'll be penniless 'til your last breath." He wiggled the knife out of the wood and cut another piece of steak, swirled it around in the juices, and popped it into his mouth.

"Thanks for the reality check," Kash replied, before getting up and walking towards the front door. He stopped at the lectern to pick up his fedora as the host bid him farewell.

Chapter 2

The rain had finally ended. Kash hustled across the street to the theater.

A '69 Chrysler 300 sedan, adorned in yellow city-cab attire, sat parked in front of the box office. It was an odd-looking beast. Wide, black tires were mounted on glossy, knock-off spoke rims. The engine idled roughly, sputtering through its dual Cherry Bomb mufflers.

Kash advanced towards the ticket window, half-covered by a flyer that read "Two-Dollar Admission, Free Popcorn and Soft Drink—Our 60th Anniversary Special." He leaned close to the slotted metal vent. "What's starting?"

"*Le Mans* in about five minutes."

He dropped two bucks into a half-cup in exchange for a ticket.

"Don't forget to pick up your complimentary bag of popcorn and soft drink," the attendant added.

"Thanks." Kash shifted his attention back to the cab and squinted at the name JELLY stamped on the vanity license plate.

The engine shuddered as the driver continued to give it shots of gas to keep it from stalling. Kash moved towards the front passenger door and knocked on the tinted glass. It opened a crack.

"Having troubles?"

"Just keeping her warmed up," rumbled a deep baritone voice from the cabin.

"These old Chryslers don't run well in damp weather."

"I know."

"You might want to check your distributor cap for moisture."

"It's on my checklist."

"How busy are you tonight?"

The cabby slurped through a straw. "Right now, I'm just chillin'."

"You think you'll be here for a while?"

"Maybe. It's hard to say."

"I'll leave you a deposit if you'll stick around."

"Money talks, my man. How much you got?"

He reached into his denim pocket, pulled out a money clip, and slipped a one-hundred-dollar bill through the opening.

"Wow, you must really need a ride. Not planning on robbing the place, are you?"

"Not this time."

"Good, 'cause you won't get much, and this ain't no getaway car."

"I'm headed inside to catch a flick," Kash said, adjusting the brim on his fedora.

"Which one?"

"*Le Mans.*"

"Ah man, good choice. Steve McQueen is the king of cool. *White Lighting* is my favorite though. Saw it three times already."

"Who doesn't like Burt Reynolds?" Kash asked, anxious to leave and go find a good seat inside. "Just be sure to stick around."

"Me and Ben Franklin aren't going anywhere." He flipped a switch from inside the cockpit that disabled the glowing taxi light mounted on the rooftop of the sedan.

"Terrific. I'll see you in a bit."

Chapter 3

It was just minutes before sunrise and a fading moon and starlit sky cast ghostly images of a mountainous skyline.

In the valley below, headlights from the Chrysler sedan illuminated a paved roadway that zigzagged through the natural beauty of the once-virgin landscape. Chugging along over the steep inclines, its tires squealed through each hairpin turn.

Jostled out of sleep, Kash awoke to a headliner pierced with cigarette burn holes. Slouched low in the backseat, he listened to the growl of the engine. The cabin reeked of popcorn and cigar smoke. It made him nauseous.

Sitting up, he eyed the driver—a large, muscular African-American with a shaved head and two silver earrings in his right ear. A sleeveless shirt fit tightly over his chiseled upper body.

"Well, good morning," the man said, sucking on a half-lit stogie while peering at his passenger in the rearview mirror.

"Right," Kash replied in a groggy tone. He glanced out the side window to observe the early morning sun as it started to cross the horizon.

"You fell asleep as soon as you hit the backseat."

"Thanks to the comfort of your sofa."

The driver laughed as he braked softly, approaching another turn. Kash lost his hold, falling sideways in the back seat as the vehicle leaned into the corner. A collection of loose kernels and vintage automobile magazines strewn across the floor collided with his feet. Straightening himself, he grabbed an issue of *Hot Rod* and examined the cover. It was dated February 1966.

"Did you get your fill?"

"Oh, yeah," Kash said, steadying himself through the turns by holding onto the front headrest. "I saw each one, couldn't resist. I hope you didn't mind."

"Not at all. I never had one customer all night."

"That's odd."

"Not really. I fell asleep."

"That'll do it." Kash glanced at the fare. "Your meter not working?"

"It's broken."

"How do you keep track of the cost?" He flipped a few pages, intrigued by the photographs.

"I don't."

"Maybe you ought to get that fixed?"

"Yeah, one day."

"Passengers will think your cab is out of order."

"It is."

Kash stopped scanning the pages to peer up at the driver. "Are you kidding me?"

"No sir," the man replied, glancing into the rearview. "In fact, I'm not really a cabby either."

"Then what do you call yourself?"

"An entrepreneur."

"And what about this fine automobile?" Kash asked, raising an eyebrow.

"A prop. I'm in the entertainment business. You know, promotional gigs."

"Uh-huh," Kash said, before checking to see if his money clip was still in his pocket. Relieved, he resumed flipping pages. "Working for the theater?"

"For anyone that'll pay me."

"Sounds like a tough way to earn a living."

"Yeah, it can be if you don't know how to play the game. The theater gigs are chump change, but the movie business—that's where the money is. I can pull a grand a day."

"You do many of those?"

"Unfortunately, I don't. Most of them are already set up with the larger players. Guys who have a huge inventory of classics. Maybe fifty to a hundred vehicles or more."

"I wouldn't think there'd be a big demand for a '69 yellow cab."

"There's not, but this is not my only set of wheels. I have a '55 Ford pickup, '57 Cadillac, and '66 Mustang convertible I'm restoring."

Kash looked up with interest.

"Also got my eye on a '40 Ford coupe. But I don't quite have the funds yet."

"Sounds like you know a bit about old cars."

"I was a mechanic and bodyman years ago, in the good old days before they added computers to cars. Wouldn't touch a new vehicle today if they paid me. They're a whole different breed, if you know what I mean."

"I do." Kash tossed the magazine aside. "What's your name?"

"Jelani. I use to own Christie's Speed Shop on the east side. Maybe you heard of it?"

"Don't think so."

"It burned down back in the '80s. I lost everything."

"Sorry to hear that."

"Ah, that's life. It gives and it takes."

"Jelani. That's a name you don't hear too often."

"It means 'mighty and powerful.' Do I fit the bill?" He cast a wide smile that reminded Kash of a pumped-up Cheshire cat.

"No argument here. Mind if I call you Jel for short?"

"I'm cool with that. And you are?"

"Thomas Kash. Like Johnny, but spelled with a 'K.'"

"Nice to meet you."

Looking at his watch, Kash sighed.

"You in a hurry?"

"A bit."

"What's the rush, if you don't mind me asking?"

"I have a hot date and I don't want to keep her waiting."

"My momma always said, a girl's only worth keepin' if she'll wait for you."

"Your mother was a smart woman."

"Yes, she was." Jel held up a necklace with a cross on it and kissed it.

"What do you have under the hood?"

"TNT baby. A 440, big-block."

"Is it all show and no go?"

"Hang on." He punched the accelerator. The car hesitated a second before launching off.

Kash stretched out as the sedan floated along at high speed. About a mile down the road, Jel eased up on the gas, bringing the land yacht to rest just above the posted limit.

"Not bad." Kash searched his jacket for his set of worn-out driving gloves. Once found, he put them on and worked each finger individually to ensure a snug fit with no restrictions.

"What's your lady's name?"

"Destiny."

"Sounds beautiful."

"She sure is. A real head-turner."

"Good for you, man. I hope she's one of those passionate women that cry out when you make love to her?"

"Oh," Kash chuckled, amused by the direction of the conversation. "She squeals through almost every gear."

"Squeal?" Jel pondered with envy. "Sounds like a keeper."

"Generally speaking, I like to warm her up a bit, before I lay into her." Kash flashed a devious grin.

"Hey man, whatever turns your crank. I know I could never do that to my ex." He shook his head in disbelief, then lowered the driver's side window and tossed out his cigar. The wind whistled through, bringing with it a fresh smell of early morning dew.

Kash leaned forward and stared out the front window at the hood that was as long as a diving board. "You sure do like the full-size models, don't ya?"

"Oh, you got it, man. Something with a bit of meat on the bone. Like Campbell's Soup says, 'mmm, mmm, good'."

The conversation helped Kash take his mind off his troubles, but the ride was almost over. "You might want to slow down. My stop is coming up, right where there's a For Sale sign on the property," he said, navigating.

Ahead, on a densely-treed lot, a stone driveway emerged. The Chrysler veered into the laneway, narrowly missing two granite Ford Cobra statues. As the car lurched to a stop, Kash put on his shades, pulled out his money clip, and handed over two crisp one-hundred-dollar bills.

"Whoa, hold on there a minute. Let me give you some change."

"Keep it. Put it towards that old Ford you got your eye on."

"Are you sure? You paid a lot for a one-way ride."

"It was worth every dollar." Kash snatched up the *Hot Rod* magazine. "Mind if I keep this?"

"Be my guest." Jel folded the bills in half and stuffed them into his shirt pocket. "I can take you up to the house if you want."

"Not necessary. Right here is just fine." Kash tossed open the door and hopped out.

Lowering the driver's side window, Jel stuck his head out. "Thanks for the extra coin."

"Don't mention it."

"Do you want me to stick around in case your lady friend has left?"

Kash scanned the scenery. "No, I got a feeling she's waiting for me inside." He caught a glimpse of the spider tattoo on Jel's forearm. "Thanks for the lift."

"Wait a minute." Jel pulled out a business card. "Here. In case you ever need my services. Maybe this lady of yours has a friend?"

"I'm afraid not. She doesn't get out much these days," Kash said, reaching into his back pocket to exchange cards.

Jel read the words aloud: "Kash and Kars. Restoration Specialists and Motorcar Auctions."

"If you can still swing a wrench, stop by and see me. I could use a guy like you."

"I probably wouldn't get past the interview."

"You already have."

"Right," he replied with a tone of sarcasm in his voice, before planting a foot on the brake and plunking the gear shifter into reverse.

"Just 'cause you're an ex-con doesn't mean you don't deserve a second chance."

"What are you talking about?"

"Or is that fake, too?" Kash pointed to the tattoo.

"No, it's real man, but I don't hotwire cars anymore."

"You're dating yourself, Jel," he chortled. "People don't use the term 'hotwire' anymore. They 'boost' cars nowadays."

"What I mean to say is that I'm on the straight and narrow."

"That's why I'm offering. Just come by my shop and check it out for yourself." He tapped the roof of the car as the cab rolled out with Jel shaking his head.

Before the wheels could make it to the road, Jel stuck his head out the window one more time. "Are you sure you're not pulling my leg?"

"I wouldn't do that, Jel. You're too damn big."

Chapter 4

The laneway traveled around massive red oaks, giving Kash that familiar homecoming feeling. The old wooden swing that his daughter played on as a child still hung from the tree.

As he rounded a corner, his daughter's '94 Jeep Renegade sat parked in front of his sprawling, modern-day Ponderosa. A large canine of German Shepherd and Labrador mix lay stretched out and asleep on a mat by the front entrance. The dog opened its eyes and squinted, delivering a dull growl.

"It's me Indy." Kash removed his glasses and Indy wagged his tail. "Look what I brought you." He held up a biscuit drawn from his pocket and tossed it nearby.

Indy moved stiffly from his resting spot. It was clear that he had become a victim of time as his whiskers and chin were now white. Kash slipped a hand under the shoe mat and retrieved a house key. He unlocked the front door and stepped inside, letting in the sun's rays.

Leaving the key on the kitchen counter, he headed through the living room, and down the hall.

"I haven't got anything," said a female voice. Startled, Kash made his way to the master bedroom. His daughter, a slender brunette, lay on her side, deep asleep, curled up with a teddy bear, appearing almost child-like. Sandra was his only child and the love of his life. He gently pulled her sheets and comforter up over her, then quietly backed out of the room, closing the door behind him.

Descending a wooden spiral staircase into a finished basement, his pace was sure and precise. He grasped the brass handles of a set of French doors and turned the levers. The spindles recessed past the strike plate and made a familiar clicking sound that gave him goosebumps. Kash entered the garage as, one by one, rows of bright lights illuminated the nearly empty surroundings.

The silhouette of his tall stature filled the entrance as he paused to recall the stunning collection he once owned long ago.

Hangers sat empty where porcelain dealership signs once hung from the ceiling like fruit from a tree. Gone too were the large, restored gravity-fed gas pumps and service station memorabilia. In one corner, there should have been an old Wurlitzer jukebox beside several old-fashioned pinball machines, but they had long since disappeared and been replaced with a shipment of moving boxes.

At his side, a ping pong table occupied the floor where a handful of vintage Indian motorcycles were formerly displayed. On a high shelf, now empty and cobwebbed, was a spot for countless mascots from the most revered automobile manufacturers of the early twentieth century.

Closing his eyes, he could picture his cars. A burgundy '67 Jaguar E-type roadster parked between a yellow '70 426 cubic-inch Hemi

'Cuda with a black vinyl roof, and a bright red '67 Lamborghini Miura. The second row exhibited his '65 Aston Martin DB5 convertible, finished in British racing green, sitting next to his silver '55 Porsche Spyder, like the one James Dean was killed in.

In his imagination, he wandered about the room, dragging a finger across the hood of his white '62 Mercedes-Benz 300SL roadster just to feel the contour of its sweeping design, before stopping to close the hood on a bright orange '70 Boss 429 Mustang. He mentally tapped the roll bar on his blue and white '65 Ford Daytona Cobra as he strolled on by and pulled the cover over the front end of his '48 Tucker finished in its original waltz blue.

Opening his eyes, disappointment washed over him as he let the magazine slip from his fingertips and land on the floor. It was all gone except a few sentimental items like his father's beloved '49 Merc resting on jack stands, covered by a half-inch of dust. Leaning against the fender was Kash's own Flying Mercury bicycle with deflated balloon tires. He gently pulled the bike back onto its kickstand.

Next to it, a tarp was draped over another automobile, revealing curves that could only belong to one exclusive breed. With his heart fluttering, Kash grabbed the cover and whipped it back, exposing a stunning, chrome-finished grille. Below, a vanity license plate read DESTINY. He smiled in absolute joy, as if reunited with a long-lost flame.

After rolling off the cover and tossing it out of the way, Kash admired the sweeping lines and brilliant Rio red paint accented with arctic white coves—the unmistakable trademark of a '61 Corvette roadster. Even to someone without interest, the impeccable details of such a classic would be impossible to ignore.

Designed well before ergonomics were conceived, Kash lowered himself into the seat, carefully sliding his legs beneath the steering wheel, and closed the door. Reclining in comfort, he gazed around at the aircraft-type cockpit, enamored by the cluster of gauges, the four-speed manual transmission, and the infamous chicken bar for the faint-at-heart passenger.

His right knee brushed against the keys dangling from the ignition, practically begging him to go for it. Kash pumped the accelerator a few times, cranked over the engine, and the Vette sparked to life. He pushed a button and the white power top recessed exposing the full interior. After sliding into first gear, he gave it a shot of gas to hear that bassy, throaty V8 rumble. The sound was erotic to him. When he released the clutch, the roadster rolled gracefully forward as sensors triggered a door to raise overhead.

Once outside, Kash idled down the meandering laneway, stopping to slip on his sunglasses before hitting the road.

For the first few miles, he drove like an elderly person on a driver's exam, slowly moving through the twists and turns and abiding by every law. Motoring around a curve, the sun glimmered off the shimmering paint and brightwork.

A final look at the temperature and oil gauges proved the automobile was warmed up and ready for action. Kash licked his lips. It was time to unleash the power under the hood and have one last hoorah.

Letting loose, he throttled down a clear stretch of pavement surrounded by peaks and valleys. The high performance 283 cubic-inch, pushing over 270 horses, was a symphony of power as the speedo tipped 90 mph.

Tucked low behind the windshield to keep from losing his fedora, Kash relished the cool air blasting across his face while mesmerized by the towering escarpment flanking the highway. It was a scene of stunning perfection, soon to be interrupted by the grotesque sight of a polluted city below.

Chapter 5

A trailer sign proclaiming "Kash and Kars Classic and Vintage Motorcar Auction" stood outside the entrance of the Columbus Sports Complex in South Park, Los Angeles.

Inside the cavernous arena, media interviewed visitors pouring through the front doors who were happy to share their wish list of potential buys.

Past the turnstiles, rows of vendors prepared an array of hot foods that scented the air. Some patrons stood in line to grab a bite to eat or something cool to drink before taking a seat at the bidder's circle.

Over 100 collector cars covered the middle of the showground, spanning decades of automotive design and innovation. Intertwined by red-carpeted walkways and velvet ropes, marques were positioned strategically under high-intensity white lights.

Donnie Kars, master of ceremonies, stood at the center of it all. A tall, middle-aged man with a shaved head and a salt and pepper goatee, he was dressed dapperly in a black sports jacket, matching pants, crisp white shirt with burgundy tie, and glossy leather loafers. His radio voice resonated through the loudspeakers as he finished announcing the distinctive pedigree of a fire-engine red '57 Chevrolet Bel Air through a wireless headset.

"I have an opening bid of one-forty-five," Donnie said timidly, standing behind the lectern. He was out of his element, having to fill in last minute when the hired auctioneer failed to show. "Will someone counter at one-fifty?" He combed the viewers, spotting an elderly man wearing an awful toupee and holding a raised paddle. "Thank you, sir, I now have a top bid of one-fifty. Looking for one-fifty-five." Donnie was anxious to see another bid. "One-fifty-five!" He surfed the room, but there was no response. "Alright. One-fifty going once," he warned. "Twice," he said, with more urgency, again looking for someone, anyone. "And for the very last time—" Donnie slammed the gavel down. "Sold, to number thirty-four." He smiled humbly, having closed the fiftieth sale of the day. Despite his lack of auctioneering experience, sales were looking promising.

The buyer rose casually from his chair and waved courteously at Donnie as the Chevy drove away, making room for the next make and model.

"Congratulations, sir." Donnie gave him his well-practiced salesman's grin and waved back. "You've just added one exquisite piece to your collection."

Reverend Ray James, a Kash and Kars employee, moved sluggishly to fetch the next order. Affectionately referred to as "Rev" by his coworkers, he was in his late sixties and exhibited a black, buttoned shirt with a white minister's collar. His thinning, gray hair was brushed to one side and his well-groomed mustache was curled neatly on each end. Overweight and out of shape, he perspired heavily as he moved along.

Donnie cleared his throat and addressed the crowd. "As General Manager of Kash and Kars, it gives me great pleasure to present our feature of the day." He sounded so genuine he almost convinced himself. "Complete details on this incredible nut-and-bolt, ground-up restoration can be found in your catalog, lot number fifty-one. Please take a moment to read the incredible details of this fine specimen while it is brought up for your viewing pleasure."

Donnie gestured to Rev to shift it into high gear. "Hurry up," he mouthed silently.

Rev dismissed him with a curt shrug.

"Folks, Reverend James is not only one of our loyal staff members here at Kash and Kars," Donnie announced, trying to kill time, "but he is also the steady-handed mechanic who has fine-tuned many of these magnificent automobiles for your driving pleasure."

Amused disbelief flashed across Rev's face as he stared at Donnie. "Steady hands my ass," he murmured as a set of keys shook uncontrollably in his hand. He clenched his fist so no one would notice. It was a testament—along with his huffing and puffing—to years of drug and alcohol abuse.

"Reverend, give us all a big friendly salute."

Raising his left hand, he extended the middle finger while crossing the stage, eliciting chuckles from the spectators. He chortled with satisfaction.

Unamused, Donnie grimaced. "That's our good old joking Reverend, alright. Unfortunately, he doesn't move as fast as he used to, so we'll give him another minute."

From the corner of his eye, Donnie spotted a fellow climbing the stairs to center stage. With a lit cigarette in mouth and a glass of Scotch in hand, the short, dark-haired gentleman teetered from side to side, as though he might trip and fall at any moment. It looked like a fifty-fifty shot.

Unlike Donnie's sophisticated attire, the man modeled a bright red plaid jacket, purple pleated pants, and fresh, white sneakers. As he made it to the top step, clearly intoxicated, Donnie clenched his teeth. It was Jacques, hired to auctioneer the event and late as usual.

In the distance, the next vehicle for auction fired to life.

"Ah, ladies and gentlemen, that's the sound of our feature car on its way," Donnie said, trying to hold the attention of the crowd.

Jacques stumbled across the podium, taking a quick sip every couple of steps. Spilling a few dribs along the way, he stopped to remove his cigarette and lick up the droplets of Scotch from his sleeve. With a mix of embarrassment and dread, Donnie glared at him with swelling vexation.

"Well, finally. You made it," Donnie sighed, glancing at his Rolex. It was a quarter past eleven in the morning. He turned to face the audience, trying to keep his irritation under control. "I am now going to hand over the floor to our official spokesperson. A man whose reputation and expertise in the world of timeless automobiles is as significant as Cupid's arrow is to matchmaking. Despite his attire, which would no doubt make every used car salesman green with envy, he is as passionate about motorcars as any of us here today." A few beads of sweat ran down his forehead as Jacques walked unsteadily towards him. "Without further ado, please give a warm welcome to our friend and wannabe rock star, Mr. Jacques Poirier."

Onlookers applauded wholeheartedly as Jacques, seemingly tuckered out from the physical exertion of walking to the lectern, stood glassy-eyed. His drink was nearly gone, leaving the ice cubes to clink around. Reaching for a handshake, Donnie gripped Jacques's arm firmly, keeping him steady, and spoke into his ear. "You're over two hours late!"

"Couldn't find the bloody place," Jacques replied in his native English Jersey Channel accent. "But you know the old adage, better late than never."

Donnie stared at him. "For God's sake, wipe off that blow from under your nose and pull yourself together."

"Yeah mate, I've got it in the bag." He squinted a few times, exhaled a stream of smoke, then dusted a hand across his face.

"And get rid of that filth." Disgusted, Donnie passed over his headset and pointed to a catalog filled with sticky notes resting atop the lectern, just as Rev arrived with the highlight of the sale.

Two videographers jockeyed alongside to capture the vehicle's glorious, restored condition. The images were broadcast across the stadium on multiple big screens. The engine's unmistakable sound launched spectators out of their seats. Every eye in the place was locked on the iconic movie car.

"Just park the damn thing on the carousel," Jacques instructed, pointing to a round, flush-mounted turntable built into the floor.

Rev edged all four wheels onto it before cutting the engine. A technician standing offstage triggered the carousel into motion.

Struggling for the seatbelt release, it was a full minute before Rev could set himself free. As the door swung open, a safe exit looked impossible. "Ah, crap," he muttered, shutting the door. He hated the roundabout. It always made him nauseous.

Donnie ambled down to a chair in the front row, a reserved section, between Miss Sabrina, a young, co-op business student with a girl-next-door look, and Dr. Mullins, the Australian owner of the vehicle on the block. "Doc," as Donnie liked to refer to him, was a stocky fellow with shock white hair and thick, black-framed glasses.

Donnie nodded politely at the well-dressed aristocrat, who responded with a dubious stare. "Good morning, Doc."

"Mr. Kars," Doc responded flatly, unimpressed by Jacques's lack of professionalism.

"Going to be a good show today."

"Your man is drunk!" Doc squeezed his catalog in half.

"Who? Jacques? No, that's just theatrics."

"Nonsense! That man's intoxicated."

Miss Sabrina was drawn by Doc's sharp tone.

"Liberace wandered through a crowd with a candelabra as part of his intro to get everyone's attention. Jacques pretends he's drunk. Both get the same result. It's simply an attention-getter," Donnie argued.

"You mean he's not all liquored up?" Miss Sabrina asked.

"Well, not entirely."

"Oh, sweet Jesus!" Doc exclaimed, slapping his hands across his knees. "I spent thousands shipping my car all the way from Australia so I could get top dollar at *your* auction."

"Doc, listen to me." He patted him on the shoulder. "Jacques is not the most tactful guy. In fact, you can bet he'll manage to offend a few folks here today. He usually does."

"You mean to tell me he's like this all the time?"

"Yes, it's one big show, but when it comes to fetching top dollar for your wheels, Jacques *is* the best in the business. Like I say to all our clients, just sit back, relax, and enjoy the ride."

Jacques sat his drink on the slanted top of the stand. It began to slide. With reflexes still in check, he caught the glass before it toppled over and stared at the brownish mixture of remaining Scotch and melting ice cubes. "Ah, the hell with it," he announced, looking at it as an easy conquest and knocking it all back in one mouthful. He raised his arm in victory. "Ta-da! I'll take another, and make it a double!"

"Oh, for Pete's sake," Doc muttered.

Donnie nudged Miss Sabrina, prompting her into action. She grabbed a bottle of water from under her chair, stood up, straightened her miniskirt, and jogged up the stairs. Her firm, full breasts bounced under a clingy, light-colored blouse, completely mesmerizing the observers.

"Mercy," Jacques slurred upon seeing her.

Miss Sabrina removed the empty glass from his fingers in exchange for some H2O and strutted back to her spot as Jacques ogled every delicious inch of her. While adjusting the microphone to fit, he gazed at her buttocks as they move in rhythm with her steps.

"Nice legs. What time do they open?"

The crowd chuckled at his remark. Miss Sabrina pivoted around and responded with a one-finger salute.

"One o'clock. Alright, I'll see you then."

The quip elicited another round of guffaws from the audience.

Upon returning to her seat, she slid the glass beneath her chair, turned to Donnie, and scoffed, "He's a real charmer. Where did you find this guy?"

30

"In prison."

"That explains it."

Jacques enjoyed the last taste of his cig before extinguishing it beneath the tip of his shoe. He stood on queue as a technician from behind the stage dimmed the lights over the audience. It was showtime.

Chapter 6

A hanging spotlight shone down on the feature car. Its impeccable fresh, yellow paint, and combo red, white, and blue colors, glistened. The word "Interceptor" was spelled out across the trunk lid in crisp, white letters. The front end gave way to Nasa hood scoops, while polished mag wheels and black Renegade tires complemented the styling. Red and blue police lights mounted on the vehicle's roof flashed around the room. The presentation was stunning. Most viewers were already on their feet, taking snapshots and recording videos to capture the grand debut, while others were anxious for the bidding to start.

"Hopefully Rev put it in park," Donnie remarked.

Doc's expression grew solemn over the thought of his beloved movie car rolling off the stage.

"Yeah, like last time," Miss Sabrina recalled. "Damn near took out everyone sitting in front row."

Doc choked on his coffee.

"Easy there, Doc," Donnie said, patting him on the back.

From behind the stage, a technician operated a beam of light that encased Jacques, who was getting into character—disheveling his mop of curly, blonde hair. Squeezing his eyes and casting a devilish grin, he took the catalog and threw it down on the lectern with great force. It created a loud boom that shook the notes loose. They swooshed up in the air before descending softly at Donnie's feet. "How the hell is everybody?"

The crowd, engaged by his zany off-the-cuff routine, responded amiably.

Doc shot Donnie a stern, sidelong glare. "If my car doesn't make reserve, you can pay the shipping back to Australia."

"When it sells, I'll accept a cool thousand as an apology."

"Don't hold your breath." Doc opened his catalog to the spread on his automobile.

"Alright, where are we?" Jacques asked.

"Huh," Doc scoffed. "And *he's* supposed to be the best in the business."

"Just remember, I want my apology paid out in small denominations."

Spotting the feature turning on the carousel, Jacques caught himself. "Aha, yes. Feast your eyes on this rare example, this collectible commodity, if you will, of pure Australian testosterone." His voice thundered through the speakers as he prowled around the podium, fully commanding it. "A true piece of cinematic iconography—a 1975 Ford Falcon XB Pursuit Interceptor, driven by the one and only Mel Gibson in the original cult classic *Mad Max*." He wandered towards the front row. "How many of you have seen the movie?"

Nearly everyone waved their hands, accompanied by a few "woo-hoos" and "yeahs."

"Remember all those extreme car chases and wacky characters? The Toe Cutter, Mudguts, and that terminal psychotic, Nightrider." He broke into a crazy laugh. "What a bunch of freaks! But what else would you expect from a country that began as a penal colony? Australia's just one giant Alcatraz. Killers, kooks, and kangaroos."

Donnie sunk into his seat, gut-wrenched and embarrassed by the ethnic slurs.

"Is this your idea of a joke?" Doc's cheeks reddened as he confronted Donnie.

"It's his shtick. He's working the crowd."

"And what about Mel?" Jacques asked. "He was about twenty-two when they filmed that epic, wearing that cool jacket and tight, black leather pants, looking like he had a wombat or something trapped in there, if you know what I mean." Jacques gestured at his crotch for emphasis.

Miss Sabrina's mouth fell open in disbelief. She glanced sideways at Donnie who remained slouched in his chair.

"Chasing that villainous Nightrider in this damn thing right here!" He threw his arms out, casting his approval on it.

The bidders fired back with immediate applause.

Donnie was still unsettled by Jacques' earlier remarks. He peeked at Miss Sabrina.

"Is he always this insulting?" she asked.

"Yes, but his sell rate is phenomenal."

"Whew! We got some fans here today," Jacques said as he approached the vehicle.

"What's he doing?" Doc asked.

"I think he's going to make a jump for it," Miss Sabrina said, watching him bend his knees.

"He better not scratch the paint."

"I can't watch." She turned away.

Leaping into the air as the nose of the vehicle swung around towards him, Jacques landed against the grill with a thud as his upper body flew forward, bumping his head off the hood. A few "whoas" erupted from the audience.

"He made it," Donnie said, sighing in relief.

Jacques must have noticed Rev behind the windshield, shooting him the middle finger, but he never let on.

"Oh yeah," Jacques yelled as he slowly stood, leaning on the hood to steady himself.

Donnie tensely stroked his goatee, nearly pulling out the hairs.

"Do my eyes deceive me? Just take a look at this damn thing," he said putting his foot on the fender as the technician slowed the carousel to a halt. "Let me tell you folks, this is the most expensive sedan you're ever going to buy."

From inside the cockpit, Rev flipped on the toggle switch that activated the police siren. It only lasted a few seconds, but it was enough to startle Jacques, almost knocking him off balance. Rev chortled with gratification.

"Whoa," Jacques shouted. "Check that out!" He maneuvered to the passenger window to speak to Rev. "Crank her over and stand on it."

Rev fired up the engine and tapped hard on the accelerator causing enough torque to rock the vehicle.

"Just listen to that engine!" Jacques yelled. "That's 350 horsepower!" He wandered around the podium as the viewers chanted "Mad Max." He egged on the spectators, cupping his ear as if saying "I can't hear you."

Emboldened, Donnie straightened up in his chair. "That a boy. Reel 'em in."

A clip from the original movie played across the video screens in the arena. Images cast the Falcon chasing down a stolen Pursuit Special.

Jacques spoke in sync with the clip. "*I am the Nightrider. I'm a fuel-injected suicide machine. I am a rocker, I am a roller, I am an out-of-controller!*" Every enthusiast went wild, clapping and whistling, fully enamored by his antics.

The scene ended with a climactic explosion as the villain and his female passenger died in a blazing fireball. The screens then faded to a shot of Jacques posturing on stage, awaiting recognition.

Donnie rose from his chair, applauding as viewers followed suit, but Doc remained seated and unstirred.

Having the bidders right where he wanted them, Jacques worked another angle. "Right now…" he said in a serious tone, "…is the only time you can buy this incredible piece of movie history—a multiple award showcase winner that has been meticulously restored. Let's get serious and start the bidding off at seven-fifty." The room went silent. "Seven hundred." He looked around, dabbing his brow with a neatly folded handkerchief drawn from his pocket. "Six-fifty." He was getting frustrated. "Bloody hell, are you people alive?" He glanced at their reserved expressions knowing all too well that the bidders were playing hardball. "Alright, last chance before I pass on this once-in-a-lifetime opportunity altogether," he threatened.

The audience moaned as Doc's face tightened with frustration.

"C'mon then, let me see those hands high in the air. This is *the* car everyone here wants to own and you're not going to steal it for a quarter million. So, let's open up our wallets." It looked like he spotted a bidder. "Okay, I have a starting bid of five hundred thousand, now five-ten," he said, pointing to infinity. "Five-twenty, thank you."

"Wait a minute," Miss Sabrina gasped, scanning the multitude of potential buyers. "I don't see any bids."

"It's called chandelier bidding," Doc whispered, eavesdropping on the conversation.

"But isn't that unethical."

Donnie shrugged his shoulders. "But effective."

"In sales, a certain amount of dishonesty is always expected. Isn't that right, Mr. Kars?"

Leaning over to whisper in Miss Sabrina's ear, Donnie was irked. "Gimme a break. Like he got rich from being honest."

Attendees started bidding in earnest and a minute later the value climbed to six hundred and forty thousand dollars.

"Six-fifty," shouted a well-endowed blonde dressed in gaudy jewelry, sitting five rows back.

"I love it when someone yells out a bid, it makes my job that much easier. I now have six hundred and fifty thousand dollars from this lovely lady," Jacques said, pointing. "Ma'am, you're my kind of woman. Were you a model at one time?"

The blonde stood up and flipped her hair. "I was an exotic dancer." She had everyone's attention.

"Well, may I ask what interest you have in purchasing this fine automobile?"

"I want something that can take me from zero to two hundred in less than five seconds."

"Perhaps you should buy a scale."

A mixture of laughter and giggles broke out.

"Oh, screw you!"

"I may take you up on that offer after several more drinks."

Several paddles shot up into the air. He knocked them off as if they were shooting targets. "I now have a top bid of six hundred and eighty thousand dollars, and to be quite honest, we still have a way to go on this one."

A high-pitched whistle shot across the room where, six rows back, a young cowboy stood up near the aisle to make his presence known. He had on a Stetson hat and looked like he had just sauntered out of a Marlboro ad. "That car's mine. So everyone else can quit now and go home."

"Well, it looks like the competition just showed up," Jacques replied as the bid was hiked another ten grand.

The cowboy remained standing as if to dominate the room. He was cocky, maybe too sure of himself, but just the way Donnie liked them at auction.

"Who will take it to seven hundred thousand?" Jacques scanned the room and spotted an elegant, leggy, blonde twenty-something. She was wrapped in tight, black jeans, perched atop six-inch heels, and standing beside an elderly man in a wheelchair. He appeared to be clinging to life, connected to an oxygen tank with tubes shoved up his nostrils. Her fingers caressed the elderly man's skeleton-like hand. She raised her paddle.

"Please tell me you're his granddaughter, for heaven's sake."

The woman flashed a large diamond ring.

"Uh-huh. Okay. Seven hundred thousand!"

The cowboy stared on, angered and appearing ready to jump over the seats to wring the neck of the old man and his trophy wife.

Donnie leaned forward for a view of the high bidder. Miss Sabrina followed suit.

"That's Bob Redding," Donnie said.

"Let me guess, multi-millionaire?" Miss Sabrina replied.

"Nope. Billionaire."

"And the gold digger?"

"Wife number four, I believe."

"Looks like he's already got one foot in the grave."

"Yeah, and the other on a banana peel," Doc interjected.

Jacques dabbed more sweat from his forehead. "The bid is now seven hundred thousand dollars, courtesy of 'Ol' Man River' sitting near front row."

"Uh-oh," Donnie said.

"What's wrong?" Miss Sabrina asked.

"Redding's our biggest client and we don't want any insults fired at him." Donnie pulled a Sharpie from his shirt pocket and grabbed Doc's catalog off his lap. He wrote "BOB REDDING $$$" on the back in big letters, stood up from his seat, and got Jacques's attention, who acknowledged him with a nod.

Donnie tossed Doc's catalog back into his lap. The corner edge scored him in the groin. Doc cried out, almost doubling over in pain as Donnie whistled at Gordy King, who was standing on the sidelines.

Gordy was an intimidating ring man, a go-getter with over forty years of experience in the auction business, and a hired gun whose sole purpose was to amplify bidding wars.

Dressed in black pants and a white monogrammed shirt, he had deep facial lines, a pickled nose, and fine strands of slicked-back hair that made him look like an old-school gangster. With a single finger point from Donnie, Gordy carved his way through the seated bidders. By the time he greeted the cowboy, he'd summed up his adversary as easy prey.

Overwhelmed by all the excitement, the cowboy was a target for someone like Gordy, who was good at stick-handling people. There was a short exchange of words before a bid was fired back to the stage.

"I've got seven hundred and ten thousand!" Jacques confirmed with eagerness. "Now back to you Mr. Redding at seven-twenty."

"Watch this," Donnie murmured to Miss Sabrina as he pointed towards Redding. "Look how he communicates."

Redding moved his fingers to signal his wife. She dutifully made another bid.

"Seven hundred and twenty thousand." Jacques belted out as Redding's wife raised the bid. "Thank you, love. Now I need seven-thirty. Seven-thirty."

"Lost his speech a few years ago from a stroke," Donnie said softly.

"I can't believe he's still buying. He looks like he should be purchasing a burial plot, not another automobile," Miss Sabrina responded.

Gordy was persistent, having the ear of the cowboy all to himself. "If you want those wheels, boy, now's the time to show no fear." That was all it took to push the cowboy on. Gordy confirmed with a resounding, "Yup!"

Again, Redding had his wife bid.

"Seven hundred and forty thousand!" Jacques exclaimed.

The attention bounced between Redding's wife and the cowboy.

"It's only money, boy. They print it every day," Gordy said, grinning with yellow-stained teeth. He garnered another tender at seven hundred and fifty thousand dollars.

The bid increments quickly dropped from ten thousand to five thousand—a sign that things were beginning to slow down—though Redding was in the lead at seven seventy-five. It was up to the young man to counter.

"Boy, you can't turn back," Gordy said. "You're too darn close. You fold now and you just let some broad and a crippled old man kick your ass empty-handed all the way back home!"

The cowboy, fuming, removed his ten-gallon hat and slapped it across his knee before smashing it back down on his feathered, blond hair. Sweat was soaked through the armpits of his t-shirt. "Alright," he said. "I'll go up another five."

Gordy shouted out another resounding bid at seven hundred and eighty thousand. He shot his fingers into the air as if making a touchdown at the Superbowl.

Jacques addressed Redding's wife. "Seven eighty-five?" he asked her point-blank.

Redding gave the signal once more to his spouse and the bid was made.

"Seven hundred and eighty-five thousand dollars, ladies and gentlemen," Jacques hollered to the cowboy. "Give me seven-ninety!"

"This sounds like the perfect recipe for buyer's remorse," Miss Sabrina said.

"Happens all the time," Donnie replied.

The cowboy was disgusted. He stepped closer to the front of the stage as Gordy tagged alongside, still working him.

"You're near the peak of the mountain, son. Time to give it all you got!"

Rattled, the cowboy booted an empty chair out of his way, toppling it over with a bang.

"Think about this for a second. There's only one *Mad Max* Interceptor, and it's right here, right now," Gordy argued. "Just make it seven-ninety and let's get on with it." He slapped him on the shoulder.

The young man contemplated for a few seconds, his face uncertain. "Um, alright, I'll give it one more shot."

"Atta boy." Gordy spun on his heels and shouted out the high bid.

"Seven hundred and ninety thousand dollars," Jacques hollered. He gestured to have the vehicle removed. Rev cranked over the engine and it sparked to life flexing its V8 muscle.

Redding closed his eyes and breathed in the exhaust, like it was a drug to him. One that he could not refuse. He nudged his wife and she raised the bid for the umpteenth time.

"Seven hundred and ninety-five thousand dollars," Jacques yelled out as he held up his fists. "I need an even eight hundred!"

Gordy was out of convincing lines as the cowboy threw down his hat in defeat.

Rev idled the automobile across the stage, showing it off one last time. As the vehicle exited the venue, Jacques eyeballed the cowboy conversing with Gordy. It didn't look good. Gordy shook his head in dismay. Jacques shifted his attention to Donnie who gestured with a thumbs down. The reserve was still in effect and a forfeit of the sale would be a major loss for the company.

"It's time to sell this car!" Jacques announced.

Donnie whispered into Doc's ear. "We've hit top end. Your wheels won't make reserve at eight hundred thousand."

"Don't forget, you're paying the shipping."

"You're going to let the deal fall through 'cause the bid is five grand short."

"I might," Doc replied.

Donnie thought that Doc was bellyaching over peanuts. "Tell ya' what, I'll drop half-a-point on the commission if you lift the reserve."

"There's still a chance it could make it," Doc argued. There was a hint of stress in his voice.

"Doc, the ranch hand is moseying off into the sunset. There are no more bids. You really foolish enough to let this chance slip away?"

"Seven hundred and ninety-five thousand going once…" Jacques said, glancing around the bidding area with his gavel raised.

"One point," Doc said in haste.

"No. Half. I'll move from six to five-and-a-half percent. Take it or leave it."

"Seven hundred and ninety-five thousand going twice…"

Biting her nails, Miss Sabrina waited for a response.

Donnie raised his index finger to signal Jacques to hold tight.

"And for the third and final time…" he shouted and hoisted the gavel high, keeping an eye on Donnie working his side deal.

"Alright, fine," Doc grumbled.

"Smart move." Donnie signaled the "okay."

Jacques pounded the gavel repeatedly. "Sold at seven hundred and ninety-five thousand dollars to the soon-to-be widow! Congratulations to bidder number one-zero-three."

Applause erupted to commend the new owners on their purchase. Redding smiled victoriously. The cowboy stormed out.

"This guy's a professional con artist," Miss Sabrina surmised.

"I like to think of him as a master of persuasion," Donnie replied.

"Is that what got him into prison?"

"Nope. Importing fine wines."

"Since when is that a crime?"

"When the odd bottle is filled with cocaine."

Doc rose to his feet, tossed his catalog aside, and delivered Donnie a handshake. "I'll be back. Try not to sell my seat while I'm gone."

"I would if I could," Donnie responded with a sly grin.

Miss Sabrina grabbed Donnie's arm. "That was the most intense scene I've ever witnessed."

"Darling, you haven't seen nothing yet."

"Looked like you enjoyed grinding Doc."

"It's what I do best. Besides we can't afford to lose the feature sale."

"I feel like I'm at a used car convention."

"You are. The only difference is that our clients have very deep pockets."

"Doc didn't seem too tickled."

"Trust me, he's ecstatic. He just made a lot of cash."

"Speaking of Kash, where is he?"

"Considering he's got a roadster destined for the auction in about, oh, forty-five minutes, I'd say he's probably driving to beat hell."

Chapter 7

Annoyed by the nuisance of a slowpoke, Kash signaled, rammed the shifter into third gear, and shot past a bright yellow Hennessey Venom GT Spyder. The engine screamed as the tachometer shot up like a rocket with the speedo dancing off the 100 mph mark. It was not a record, but still impressive for a nearly 60-year-old automobile.

Fast cars had always been in his blood. When he was six, his father took him to the racetrack in Mount Clemens, Michigan. It was September 3, 1951, and the place opened to some 5000 spectators.

Having once been a hunter's paradise, the new facility exuded natural beauty. A verdant, tree-lined entrance opened up to three courses—a half-mile, quarter-mile, and a figure eight.

Food concessions lined the perimeter, adjoined by a large atrium where servers sold ice-cold beer faster than they could stock the coolers. Near the grandstand were a kids' playground and a sprawling picnic area shaded by enormous oak trees.

Down at the pits, race cars underwent last-minute checks as revving engines rang out for miles. Arriving early, Kash and his father got a chance to see their favorite driver, hometown hero Bela Kolyok, dubbed "Billy the Kid" by his fans. Billy was a highly-regarded daredevil, having competed all over the country. He had an insatiable appetite for victory, a reputation for unnerving stamina, and one heck of a bad temper.

Tom Kash Sr., a tall, handsome, ex-Navy vet, had brought along a pair of World War II German U-boat binoculars to catch all the action up close. "Keep these by your side and never take your eyes off them," he advised his son. "And don't lend them to anyone. They're from the war you know."

Throughout the day, there were a few fender benders, one rollover, and more than a few drunken spectators spilling their beverages with every arm-raising cheer.

By the time the race was over, it was difficult to distinguish any of the drivers behind all the dirt and grit. One by one, they pulled into the pits and removed their helmets and goggles, leaving ghostly white patches around their exhausted eyes.

As visitors left in droves, Kash wallowed in the experience. It was the coolest thing he'd ever seen, and it fueled his newfound passion for racing.

Attending the track became a father-and-son event season after season, but it was the summer of '57 that forever changed his life.

Riding home from school, he made a triumphant, fast-sliding entry into the driveway on his Flying Mercury bicycle, homework tightly strapped behind him. His father was finishing a tune-up on the family's '49 Merc.

A mere two miles from their home, every audible nuance that echoed from the track added to his curiosity.

"Dad! Do you hear that?" He pulled alongside the family hauler.

His father was closing the hood. "Hear what, son?" he asked, teasing.

"Someone's doing laps, and the next race isn't until tomorrow night."

He listened for a moment. "Could be practice runs."

"Can I ride over and see?"

His dad removed a shop rag from his back pocket and began wiping the grime off his arms. "We can get there faster in the Merc. Go put your bike away and tell your mother we'll be home for dinner in about an hour."

After wheeling his bicycle inside the garage, Kash flew up the porch steps of his parent's postwar bungalow and shouted through the screen door. "We'll be back in a bit, mom," he yelled, knowing darn well his father usually underestimated his time.

"What?" his mother cried out from the kitchen over the rattle of pots and pans.

Kash ignored her for fear of losing valuable time. He zipped back to the car as his father fired up the engine. Seconds later, they headed off, squealing out of the driveway, leaving behind a cloud of blue smoke.

Upon their arrival, the track lay quiet. Rain clouds were settled on the horizon as the pair headed quickly across the empty grounds with

Kash clutching his father's beloved binoculars by its thin, leather strap wrapped tightly around his hand.

At the pits, they discovered a handful of mechanics dressed in beige coveralls. One was changing tires on a car, another was hammering out a dented quarter-panel, and a few were making engine repairs.

Kash stood mesmerized as the binoculars dangled from his shoulder, ready to be slipped off at any moment.

"Here, let me take those before you drop them."

He passed them to his father while shifting his eyes from one crewman to the next.

"Hey, dad. There's Billy's race car!" He pointed to it. The hood was propped open and a fender apron lay over the side.

A mechanic rummaging through a nearby tool chest looked up, taking notice of two unfamiliar faces. He was a short man in his forties with a wind-tunnel-tested pompadour hairdo. A lit cigarette dangled from his bottom lip. Stitched into the upper-left side of his coveralls was his name, Smokie. He ambled towards them with a noticeable limp. "Can I help you fellas?"

"My son just wanted to find out what all the commotion was about. We didn't mean to bother anyone."

"Practice runs." He approached Kash. "And what's your name?"

"Thomas Kash Jr., sir. I'm Billy the Kid's biggest fan!"

"Is that right? Well, how would you like to meet him?"

"Are you kidding? That would be great! That is if it's alright with my dad…" He peered up at his father with large, solemn eyes—a tactic that often resulted in getting his way.

"I guess I can make an exception this one time," his father joked, barely suppressing his own excitement.

"Hey, Billy," Smokie shouted.

"Yeah. What is it?" Billy asked with his thick, Hungarian accent. He was working beneath the undercarriage, completely out of sight.

"There's a young fella here that claims he's your biggest fan. Says he's got to meet you." Smokie patted the youngster on the shoulder before returning to his work.

Billy wiggled out from under his race car and stood up to catch sight of his guests.

He was shorter than Kash expected, but it was definitely Billy the Kid. He had dark, wavy hair and a thick, barrel-chested frame—resembling that of a wrestler. There was also something unique about him, Kash thought. He had a smile that made you feel welcome right off the bat.

"Nice to meet you, young man." Billy strode over and extended a hand as big as a shovel.

Kash braced himself for a bone-crushing introduction, but Billy was gentle with him.

"I'm Tom Kash," his father interjected, seeing his son completely starstruck.

"Bela Kolyok, but you can call me Billy."

The two shook hands firmly.

Aside from the odd smear of grease and oil, Billy's white-and-blue pinstriped coveralls made him all the more striking.

"You'll have to excuse Thomas. He's a little overwhelmed, meeting his hero in person."

"Is that so?" Billy said with interest.

Kash finally untied his tongue. "Is there any chance I could see your wheels?"

"For sure, come check it out."

Finished in rich burgundy and resting on four large Firestone tires sat Billy's Indy car, which had taken him to victory just two years prior. On the track, it was a beast, but here in the pits, Kash thought, it seemed unpretentious. "Wow!" he gushed. "A real Kurtis Kraft 500C front-engine roadster, dad."

Smokie hobbled over and removed the apron off the fender as Kash began his inspection of the vehicle.

"That she is, son."

"Yes, young Thomas, that's very good," Billy said. "What else can you tell me?"

He examined the chassis. "Well, it has a fabricated, box section tube frame. Wheelbase, 96-inches. Overall weight, less driver, around 1800 pounds."

Billy remained intrigued. "And what about the heart of the machine?"

Kash glanced at the motor and came to a conclusion. "It's an Offenhauser, 270 cubic-inch inline 4, rated at 380 horsepower with dual overhead cams sporting 16 valves per cylinder head. Fuel is fed through a Hilborn injection system. The transmission is a 2-speed, modified Model A Ford."

Smokie shook his head. He was gobsmacked as his cigarette nearly fell out of his mouth. "Ain't ever heard anything like it. How old are you?"

"I just turned twelve."

It was a moment of splendor as Kash entertained them with his knowledge.

"You sure know your stuff," Billy said.

"Junior lives and breathes cars."

Billy was poised in thought. "Anything else you want to point out?"

"Just one thing: the cockpit looks kinda small."

"Yes, it's a tight fit," Billy chortled. "Hop in and see for yourself."

"Just don't bump anything," his father advised.

"Don't worry, he can't hurt a thing." Billy offered him a hand.

After climbing into the cockpit, Kash shifted his butt around in the seat, mimicking the G-forces of the open-wheeled car as it moved through imaginary bends, while making engine sounds.

"Here, you'll need a helmet and goggles at those high speeds," Billy placed his own on Kash's head.

"Congratulations on last week's race," Tom said to Billy.

"Thank you."

"You've had two consecutive yearly wins. Going for a third?"

"I'm going to try, but we'll see how it plays out."

The sounds from the cockpit were getting louder and drawing more attention from onlookers.

"She sure is an amazing feat of engineering." Tom nearly drooled over the aerodynamics of the race car.

"Yes, part of winning is having a great machine and a great mechanic. That's why I've got Smokie to take care of her," Billy said loud enough for Smokie to hear and respond with a nod. "What's this?" Billy asked Tom. "An old pair of field glasses?"

"A war souvenir. Off a German sub." Tom handed it over.

"You served?"

"I did. I was a gunner on a PT boat in the English Channel. But, nowadays I'm only firing lead from a pencil."

"I see," Billy replied. He pointed them towards the dark clouds fast approaching, positioning his finger over the focus ring while peering through the eyepiece. "Very nice." He carefully returned them. "You know the Russians have invaded my country."

"Hungary."

"Yes, these damn communists. They're the world's greatest disease."

"I agree."

"You know I came to America so I could have a better life."

"Well, I'd say you're living the dream."

"I am," Billy replied before returning his attention to Kash. "And are you living yours, young Thomas?"

Removing Billy's helmet and goggles, Kash pivoted around. "I am now."

"Perhaps one day you will capture the checkered flag."

"I sure hope so."

"Maybe then we won't have to pay admission," his father said with a chuckle. "The cost is starting to take a toll on dad's pocketbook."

"Is that so?" Billy asked. "You must come here a lot?"

"Are you kidding? My father's been following your career since you first started driving Midget Car."

"Oh, that was a long time ago." Billy laughed. "You *must* be my biggest fans."

"I think it's time we let Mr. Kolyok get back to work, son. He's a very busy man."

"Alright, dad." Kash passed off the safety gear to Billy before hopping out of the cockpit.

"We really appreciate your time. Junior will be talking about this for weeks."

"It's my pleasure, but before you go, I'd like to ask if the cost of admission will be holding young Thomas back from attending any future races?"

"Well, no, not at all." Tom felt embarrassed by his earlier remark. "I just want him to realize that money doesn't grow on trees, that's all."

"I understand completely, but perhaps I could make a business proposition?"

"Oh, what do you have in mind?"

Billy bent down, hands resting on his knees, and faced Kash. "Young Thomas, have you ever had a job?"

"I had a paper route last year."

"Excellent. May I ask, did it pay very much?"

"No. It wasn't a union job or anything like that."

Billy chuckled. "I like his sense of humor."

"Are you offering my son a job?"

"I am." Billy stood up to address Tom. "I had a young boy helping clean up after each race, but he moved on a few months ago with other commitments. Perhaps young Thomas could fill the vacancy."

For Kash, it was a once-in-a-lifetime opportunity. He stared at Billy in disbelief.

"I would pay him of course, plus he can watch the races from the pits for free."

"Really? I could watch the races from here?"

"Absolutely. You'd be one of the crew."

Kash stood with his mouth agape, eyes wide open.

"Well, I don't know." Tom rubbed his jaw.

"Dad, this is a once-in-a-lifetime opportunity!"

"Now quiet, Thomas," his father replied, sternly.

"That's okay, he's just excited," Billy said. "The thought just came to mind, really. I saw his enthusiasm and thought maybe young Thomas would like to be around all those things a boy finds himself so passionate about."

"Don't get me wrong. Junior loves automobiles and racing, but I'm not so sure his mother would approve."

"Oh, please, dad," Kash cried. "This would be a dream job, not like work at all."

Billy and Tom laughed together.

"Alright." His father said. "But, we may have to break this one to your mother kind of gently. She's never been too keen on motorsports."

"Then it's settled," Billy proclaimed with a grand smile. "You can start after school, say four o'clock. Now, if you'll excuse me, I've got to prepare for tomorrow's race."

"Of course," Tom remarked.

Billy cordially shook hands with both of them one last time before heading off.

On the ride home, Kash contemplated his good fortune. The significance of securing a foothold alongside Billy seemed as equally important to him as it did to his father.

"Well, son, you've been given a great opportunity. You'll need to prove yourself. But first, let's hope we can convince your mother."

His father's statement was a painful reminder that his mother still carried clout. She wasn't likely to leave her son's safety to a bunch of "grease-monkeys," as she liked to call them.

"Maybe we'll stop and pick up a dozen roses." His father winked at him.

"Better throw in a box of chocolates," Kash suggested, his voice trembling with unease.

His mother was no pushover. Growing up on the shores of Courtright, Ontario, she was a farm girl with three older brothers. Once, in the middle of winter, she'd arm-wrestled the eldest on a bet. The wager—a week's load of laundry done on an outdoor washboard.

His mother won.

The rain poured down heavily as the Merc came to a halt in the driveway. Kash immediately jumped out and ran up the steps. He slipped quietly past the front door while glancing at his mother, who was busy stirring a pot on the stove while humming along to one of her favorite songs playing on the radio. She was a tall brunette, wearing a red swing dress with an apron tied around her waist.

Kash made a beeline to his bedroom as his father was making his way up the steps, flowers in hand. He crashed on the bed and lay face up, door partially open, waiting for the conversation to unfold in the kitchen.

"Love that song, Cassandra," Tom said in a raised voice as the storm door banged closed behind him.

"Oh, just look at these," she responded with surprise.

"Do you like them?"

"Well, of course, they're beautiful."

A boom of thunder interrupted his eavesdropping. Kash got out of bed, then crept down the hallway with butterflies fluttering around in his stomach. Poking his head around the corner, he witnessed his mother putting the roses in a vase on the kitchen table.

"But what's the occasion?"

"Big news, mother. Junior is about to enter manhood." Tom switched off the radio.

"You don't say. Where did you and Thomas head off to in such a hurry?" She busied herself rearranging each one in an orderly fashion.

"We went to the track."

"Oh. But I thought the next race didn't start till tomorrow."

Tom swaggered over, took her by the hand, and stared into her beaming blue eyes, beguiling her. He threw his arms around her and kissed her on the lips.

Kash ducked away and stayed out of sight with his body pressed up against the wall. "Gee whiz." His father was playing every angle to sweet-talk his way into a home run.

"Well, you're certainly in a good mood," she replied.

"That's because Thomas has himself a job. Starting at sixteen hundred hours tomorrow, he will be gainfully employed as one of Billy the Kid's official team members."

"Please tell me you're kidding."

"It's true."

"But he's not even a teenager."

"He will be soon enough. Besides, you should have seen him. He was completely captivated."

"What's a young boy going to do there for work?"

Kash pictured his mother's expression turning ugly and he figured his dreams would soon be torpedoed.

"What else? Push a broom, put away tools, and maybe apply some of the basic mechanics I've taught him."

"He's still too young."

"Cassandra, it's the perfect part-time job for him. It's not like he'll be behind the wheel. Well, at least not for a few more years."

"Thomas Kash Sr., have you lost your mind? Do you want your son influenced by a bunch of maniacs, risking their lives in those suicide machines?"

"You're overreacting. He'll be as safe as if he was in your own arms."

"I find that very hard to believe."

"I'm telling you it would do greater harm to hold him back. I know this is what Thomas needs. It's something he loves."

The conversation fell silent. Kash feared the worst when his mother finally spoke up.

"Alright. But anything happens to our son, it'll be World War III."

Elated, Kash threw his thumbs in the air. "Yes!" he said a bit too loud. Fearing he may be caught listening in, he scuttled back to his room.

The Hennessey barreled past, rudely awakening him from his recollection. Responding with a burst of acceleration, the roadster struggled to close the gap. Then, by a stroke of good fortune, a stoplight ahead suddenly made it anybody's game.

Braking hard, smoke rolled off all four tires as the late-model skidded to a rest. An eighteen-wheeler geared up to cross the intersection hauling a herd of pigs with their noses sticking out of the trailer.

Kash pulled alongside the supercar and stopped. The two glamorous vehicles, sitting side by side, were strikingly different. While waiting for the light to change, the Hennessey revved its engine. Not to be outdone, the vintage Corvette followed suit. It was a high horsepower pissing contest to see who had the more appealing roar.

Acting smug, Kash glanced across to the driver of the late model roadster. Anticipating some arrogant hotshot behind the wheel, he was surprised to see a beautiful brunette wearing mirrored aviator sunglasses. She smiled at him with devilish allure and perfect white teeth, tipping her shades forward so he could see her wink.

Wow, he thought, what a knockout! On the verge of making small talk, the light turned green and she sped away, spinning her rear tires and leaving him in a wake of high-octane fumes.

Captivated, he sat and watched the Hennessey reach a quarter-mile in just a few seconds before being intercepted by a police cruiser.

The wailing siren and flashing lights were enough to garner the brunette's attention, and she pulled over.

A minute later, Kash drove by casually, watching two officers question her. She glanced at him with a subtle smile as he blew her a kiss before speeding off.

Chapter 8

The vintage Corvette skirted around commuters as Kash shifted gears and accelerated through red lights and four-way stops. His excitement diminished when he drew unwanted attention from a traffic helicopter. It flew low enough for him to spot a cameraman pointing at him.

Kash slowed down and signaled for the entrance to the Columbus Sports Complex as oncoming traffic remained heavy and dawdling. He waited impatiently to make the turn, tapping his fingers on the wheel. Across from him, an old, yellow Triumph Spitfire came to a halt, holding up traffic. The driver, who had an uncanny resemblance to Nicolas Cage, waved at him to proceed.

Squinting up at the chopper and saluting, thinking he may be live on television, Kash dumped the clutch and fishtailed into the parking lot. Following the directional signs that guided collector vehicles headed to auction, he steered through a snake-like course surrounded by timeless masterpieces articulately displayed under large tents.

Around the back of the building were three loading bays—one closed, another occupied by a large transport trailer loading a few vintage motorcars, and a third attached to a ramp where Soney stood steely-eyed. In one hand he held a cigarette and a few dockets, in the other a two-way radio.

Soney's appearance was altogether low-key, just the way he liked it—faded jeans with a matching jacket, hair in a ponytail, and a white monogrammed t-shirt printed with the Kash and Kars logo. A descendent of the Ojibwa tribe, he stood six-foot-six and weighed about 300 lbs. To a stranger, he looked intimidating, but to Kash, he was a loyal, long-time friend. Soney flicked his butt outside, then nodded to him.

With a stomp on the accelerator, a stream of fuel shot through the dual four-barrel carburetors, giving the Vette more than enough horsepower to muster up the incline.

Inside the gallery, the roadster idled past a string of turnkey classics. Soney pointed to an empty space behind a black '37 Plymouth coupe where the Vette could rest before auction. He wedged a cigarette behind his ear, tore off a docket from his clipboard, and pinned it behind a wiper.

"Give her a quick rub-down." Kash cut the engine. He tossed his hat and sunglasses onto the dash.

Soney whipped out a cloth from his back pocket and began to knock off a layer of road dust from the grill. In the background, Jacques could be heard announcing the lineage of a '72 Ford Pantera on the block.

Kash rested his gloves and bomber on the passenger seat before exiting the vehicle. He took a good look around at the interior of the building. The floors were blemished with tire marks, walls were stained from smoke, and in some cases, cement pillars were gnawed down to the rebar.

The place swarmed with people of different ages and ethnicities, some staring under a hood, crawling below a chassis, or sitting in their favorite automobile.

Parked a few cars down, a silver '64 Rolls-Royce Silver Cloud III caught Kash's attention. Two young, curly blonde-haired twin boys circled the vehicle's big swooping front fenders and gallant chrome grill. It was pure British motoring royalty that couldn't have its flawless appearance spoiled by grubby little fingers.

The boys leaped onto the front bumper and gazed over the long hood. "Wow, look at this thing!" one of them exclaimed.

Whistling on his way towards the Rolls, Rev gestured for them to step aside. "Stay clear, boys. I gotta move this thing."

They sprang off the front end and scooted over to Rev before he could get inside. As he grabbed the door handle and pulled, one of the lads tapped him on the arm.

"Excuse me, sir. What kind of car is this?"

"Ah, this is a luxury automobile."

The boys nodded in unison.

"It's a Rolls-Can-Hardly," Rev replied, like he was about to unveil the most magnificent automobile on earth to the little guys. He swung open the door, about to get inside, when they seemed eager to keep the conversation going.

"We've never heard of it," one of them declared as they both contorted their faces.

"You mean you've *never* heard of a Rolls-Can-Hardly?" Rev cast an exaggerated expression of bewilderment.

Both kids shook their heads.

"Hmm," Rev tucked his fist under his chin as if to ponder. He bent towards them, and his rear end bumped the door closed. "Maybe that's because it comes from the UK."

They glanced at one another looking even more confused.

"The United Kingdom."

They still didn't seem to get it.

He responded with an eye-roll.

"But why do they call it a Rolls-Can-Hardly?" one of them asked.

"'Cause, it rolls down one hill, but can hardly get up the next." Rev burst into laughter as he playfully disheveled their hair. No matter how many times Rev told the same joke, it always brightened his day. But, the boys didn't appear to appreciate his humor and shuffled off. As the Rolls pulled away, Kash found himself encircled by a small group approving the Vette's chiseled good looks. Passersby tossed out odd remarks that made him proud: "She's a beauty," "I bet she really motors," and, "Just where in Sam Hill have you been?"

Donnie stood a few feet away, poised yet long-faced, clipboard in hand.

"Oh, it's you," Kash said. "For a second, you looked like a jealous girlfriend."

"Very funny. Did you have a great time while you were away?"

"As a matter of fact, I did. Too bad you weren't there. You could have held onto the chicken bar," he chortled before checking himself in the side mirror, sweeping his hair back and adjusting the collar on his starched, white dress shirt.

"Do you know what time it is?" Donnie asked, giving him the gears.

"Time for this pretty lady to find a new owner." He affectionately tapped the door sill.

"Are you ever going to change?"

"At my age? Not likely."

Donnie gravitated towards the roadster. "I can't believe you're going to let this one go."

"Well, a collector once told me…" Kash replied, contemplating his response.

"I hate to ask."

"There's a time to buy, and a time to sell. Knowing when is all that matters."

"And how's Sandra feel about this?"

"I don't know. I didn't ask her."

"She'll blow a gasket. She absolutely loves this car."

"It's the one her mother and I took on our honeymoon." The thought was bittersweet and it pained him to sell the cherished little sports car. "I've been thinking about how to break it to her gently, but I still don't have that part figured out." In the corner of the room, he spotted two policemen entering through a side door. Hired security guards briefly questioned them before permitting entry. "Let's go for a walk," Kash said, guiding Donnie by the shoulder as they strolled towards the auction area.

"Did you run her through all four gears?"

"More than a few times."

"How'd she shift?"

"As smooth as mashed potatoes."

"And the engine?"

"Never missed a beat."

"Great. I'll let Rev know he did a good job with the tune-up."

"Say, how is life treating the Holy Roller?"

"Like a baby treats a diaper."

"Well, maybe I can fix that."

"I doubt it. Unless you can work miracles."

"Leave it with me."

The officers were about to pass them by. They looked young enough to be rookies.

"Morning," Kash said.

The cops' name tags read "Rokeby" and "Mandaumin." They barely acknowledged him as they trooped past. Rokeby was short, dumpy, and prematurely balding. Mandaumin was a bit taller, but thin.

"I wonder what they want." Donnie watched closely.

"Who knows."

The officers approached the vintage Corvette and began inspecting it.

"Something's up," Donnie said.

"Ah, you're just paranoid. Let's keep moving." He tried to lead him away.

"No, wait a minute."

Officer Rokeby jotted down the name "DESTINY" from the license plate while Mandaumin combed the bomber hoping to discover the owner's identification.

"Okay, what'd you do this time?" Donnie shot Kash an exasperated glare.

"What do you mean? Nothing." He shrugged his shoulders, smiling mischievously.

"Dammit, Kash," he said in a deflated tone.

"What?"

"Just when things are going great, you bring an escort, and I don't mean the ones I usually see holding your arm."

"I've got a fifty that says Soney will lead them astray."

Donnie thought about it for a moment. "Alright, I'll take that bet." He reached into his pocket and pulled out two twenties and a ten.

Soney spat on a cloth to remove bug splatter from the windshield as the two officers approached him. He slowly stood up, towering over them. It was like watching a silent movie. Mandaumin's lips were flapping and Rokeby's hands gestured wildly. Soney showed no emotion, giving only a subtle nod or shrug. He then pointed outside. The two men sped off, tripping over one another.

"Just like a pro," Kash said as he snatched the money out of Donnie's hand. "Remind me to increase his bonus."

Donnie shook his head in dismay. "I just want to know one thing."

"Shoot."

"Was it worth it?"

"Darn right it was." He smiled broadly. "After five decades of ownership, why not have a little fun."

They stopped at a concession stand.

Kash dropped ten bucks on the counter. "I'll take a mushroom hamburg and a coffee," he said to an older lady wearing a hairnet who took his order. He glanced at Donnie. "You want anything?"

"Yeah, a vacation."

"That ain't gonna happen."

"Then I'll take a tea, decaf."

The woman rang in the total, then gave back his change.

"Keep it." He was happy to give away Donnie's hard-earned money.

"Thanks," she replied, tossing the coins into a Styrofoam cup marked "tips" before running off to fill the order.

"Anything else you want to share with me?" Donnie asked.

"I played tag with a lovely brunette driving a Hennessey Venom GT Spyder."

"Tag."

"Yeah."

"It's all starting to make sense now." Donnie rubbed his forehead like a headache was coming on fast. "You know the Venom happens to be one of the fastest convertibles on the planet."

"I know."

"Probably does the quarter-mile in nine seconds."

"Sounds about right," Kash said remembering how fast she took off from the stoplight. "It was great, until she got busted for speeding."

His meal and the hot drinks arrived.

"Can I get cream and sugar, please?"

"Sure," the lady replied, quickly returning with sugar packets and small cream containers.

"That's why the cops are here looking for you," Donnie said. He poured sugar into both drinks and added cream and stir sticks.

"I don't think so."

"What makes you say that?"

"She was so far ahead, I was never on their radar." Kash took a big bite of his burg followed by a swig. He sucked his fingers as the juice ran down them, before reaching for a napkin. With a lineup forming behind them, they gathered up their buys and moved along.

"Did you even come close to winning?"

"She had 1400 horsepower under the hood and I was low on fuel," Kash replied, wiping his mouth, then stirring his coffee before taking a sip. What do you think?"

"I think you got your butt kicked by a woman," Donnie said, biting his bottom lip. "Wait 'til the crew hears this one."

"Now hold on a minute." Kash jabbed Donnie's arm, eager to set the record straight.

"Hope you got her number at least."

"Well, no. The police intervened before I could."

"Tough break," he interrupted with mock sympathy, while blowing on his hot tea.

"Well, at least I got Destiny here without a scratch, and you can tell Jacques," he said, pointing to the stage, "that the engine is officially broken in." Kash took another bite.

"I'll add an addendum to the catalog before they haul you to jail." Donnie took a sip. "Any other highlights?"

"Just one. I had a brief meeting with Dugan last night."

"Oh." Donnie looked surprised. "What's he want?"

"Our company. And he's willing to pay three million for it."

"Hmm. Three million, eh? What'd you tell him?"

"I told him you wouldn't agree to it."

"That should have got a laugh," Donnie said, stirring his tea.

"It did. Then he pushed to have an answer on the spot, so I told him no—that his offer wasn't good enough."

"I bet that set him off."

"That's putting it mildly."

"Three million would get rid of a lot of worries," Donnie said.

"And likely create some new ones." Kash downed the last drops of coffee, dragged a napkin across his mouth, and discarded both in a nearby garbage container.

"If we don't make the next two payments, Dugan will bury us."

"Well then, tell me you have some good news on our stats."

"It just so happens, you're in luck." Donnie flipped a few pages from the clipboard to where he had made some handwritten notes. "About eighty-seven percent of the cars that have crossed the block have sold. If we stay on track, we'll break a record."

"That's great. And what about Jacques? How's he been behaving?"

"The usual. He showed up late, high and drunk."

"Ah," Kash said, running a hand through his hair.

"And he's been insulting the customers."

"As long as he keeps selling, I guess he can insult whoever he likes."

"I figured you'd say that." Donnie swallowed the last of his tea.

"What about the feature car? Did it make reserve?"

"No, but I convinced Doc to sell it anyway."

"You drop the commission?"

"Half a point. It sold for seven ninety-five."

"Whew! Thank God."

"No, thank me. I'm the born salesman."

"That you are. You could convince Alaskans to buy air conditioners."

"Well, there is that global warming thing."

Kash chuckled. "What else I miss?"

"A guy jacking the bids to help sell his friend's car."

"Not again."

"Yup."

"Did you sell it to the jacker?"

"You betcha. You should've seen his face." Donnie raised his hands. "Priceless."

"Who's the seller? Anybody I know?"

"I don't think so. His name is Chevelle."

"Seriously?"

"That's how it reads on the paperwork."

"Doesn't ring any bells."

"He wants us to refund his consignment fee and release his car."

"Why didn't you deal with him?"

"I tried. He said he'd only talk to you."

"Alright. Lead the way."

Chapter 9

Gazing up at the hospitality suites while en route to his temporary office, Kash stared at all the broken window panes. "Which one of these is mine?"

"None of them," Donnie replied.

"Good. You had me worried for a second."

They zigzagged across a concrete rink that was once home to many ice hockey games, dodging puddles caused by a leaky roof. The boards, glass, and overhead scoreboard had been removed long ago.

"They're going to blow this place up in about a month," Donnie said.

"That's too bad," Kash replied, noticing a row of seats missing, with only the mounting bolts left sticking out of the floor. Yellow caution tape blocked off the area.

"Not really. This whole location sucks."

"What's wrong with it?"

"For an auction, everything. The Wi-Fi connection is intermittent, making it nearly impossible to receive live internet bids, and there's not enough room inside for all the cars." Donnie balanced his footing while stepping on a sheet of plywood.

"I saw lots of room outside." Kash followed Donnie's lead.

"That costs extra. Security, tents to keep the cars sheltered. It adds up."

Their crossing transitioned to a row of narrow planks.

"You worry too much. By tomorrow morning, the only thing people will be talking about is us setting record sales." Kash stretched his arms out from his sides for balance.

"Let's not break out the champagne just yet. We've still got a few more classics to sell," Donnie mused, while entering a walkway that tunneled below a section of the stadium seating.

Kash peered up at the solid concrete walls. "I guess having a view was too much to ask."

"Yup, but I can promise you anonymity."

A line of anxious buyers stood in single file, waiting to get into the dressing rooms where staff had set up makeshift offices to finalize the paperwork. A few clients standing near a door marked Janitorial Services were making idle chatter.

"Excuse me," Donnie said, as they kindly stepped aside. "Welcome to your temporary office." He beamed with delight as if he were about to unveil a supercar. He tossed the door wide open and gestured for Kash to be the first to step inside. There, a fit Latino security guard was trying to pacify Chevelle.

"I want my car, goddamn it!"

"I told you, sir, you'll have to wait."

Kash pretended to ignore the conversation and glanced around the room. It was small, lit by two incandescent bulbs, one of which illuminated an old steel desk. The walls were lined with steel shelving and stocked with paint and solvents. Soiled overalls hung from a wooden mop resting in a battered aluminum pail. "It's the Ritz," he quipped.

The guard cleared his throat.

Kash glanced at Chevelle. "I guess you must be—?"

"The guy who wants his wheels," Chevelle shot back.

"You can leave, Diego," Donnie said, stepping out of the way for the guard to pass.

"I'm leaving an extra radio on the desk for safety," he said, looking suspiciously at Chevelle before exiting the room.

Donnie kicked the door closed.

"Well, I'll be a monkey's uncle." Chevelle swept back his slick, black hair, exposing a crevassed face and a five o'clock shadow. "I was starting to think you didn't have the guts to show up." Reaching into his pocket, he pulled out a cigarette and lighter.

"You can't smoke in here," Donnie pointed to a warning sign posted on the wall that read Highly Flammable Liquids.

Chevelle ignored him, lit up, smiled, and relished in a few puffs.

Angered, Donnie stepped forward, but Kash caught him by the arm. "It's alright." He pointed to an empty Orange Crush can sitting on the desk. "Just put your ashes in there."

Smoke spiraled up to the ceiling as Chevelle dabbed his rollup on the can. He was badass-looking, alright, Kash thought, right down to the knife-through-the-neck tattoo showing just above his collar.

"It's really you." He took another drag and exhaled. "Once America's most legendary race car driver. Now long forgotten."

72

"Have we met?" Kash estimated Chevelle to be some 20 years his junior.

"No, but I know all about you." He started to pace the floor. "I first watched you race in '73 at the Winston 500. You got hit from behind, lost control, and flipped five times."

"I was hospitalized for weeks," Kash said, taking notice of Chevelle's drab attire—ripped jeans, scuffed cowboy boots, and a faded hoodie.

"It was an ugly day for NASCAR."

"That it was."

"My old man thought you were the best thing to ever hit the circuit since Billy the Kid."

"Thanks."

"That is, until you threw it all away."

"Alright, can we move on," Donnie said, anxious to resolve matters.

"We'll get there," Chevelle replied between breaths. "I haven't even covered the highlights yet. You had it all—championships, endorsements, and a hell of a beautiful wife."

Kash was uneasy, wondering what would come out of Chevelle's mouth next.

"Then it seemed you were plagued by a series of misfortunes. They say it comes in threes. First there was Billy, then your folks, and last, but not least, your wife." He pointed directly at Kash. "That's when you gave up."

"Who the hell are you?" Kash asked, glaring.

Chevelle's eyes were dark, cold, and empty. "And look at you now. A washed-up old man working out of a broom closet."

Stepping forward, Kash confronted him head-on. "I may be old, but I'm still tough enough to drop your ass."

"Hold up, Kash!" Donnie shouted, getting between them. "We don't need any trouble."

"You best listen to your partner," Chevelle said, snickering.

Kash took a seat on the edge of the desk, folded his arms, and smirked at the bastard.

"We need to discuss how much you owe." Donnie flipped to Chevelle's paperwork. "There's a five percent buyer's premium that needs to be paid."

"I ain't the buyer." Chevelle exhaled, tossed his cigarette butt on the floor, then kicked it into the drain.

"Well, in this case you are."

"Man, you're dumber than you look." Chevelle ran his fingers through his hair.

"Let me see the paperwork." Kash reached into his pocket for a pair of reading glasses, sat them on the tip of his nose as Donnie handed over the information, and read aloud. "Lot number twenty-seven. One '68 Chevelle SS hardtop with a 396, four-speed. No reserve. Sound familiar?"

"That's my car."

"Sold to bidder number one twenty-two. Looks like the buyer registered with a valid driver's license and a credit card. Why don't you have Miss Sabrina put a charge against it for twenty-five hundred and see if it sticks," he asked, peering over his specs at Donnie. "That'll cover the commission if this guy decides to renege on the purchase." Kash returned the paperwork and put his glasses away.

"Sounds good to me," Donnie said, eager to leave.

"Wait a minute." Chevelle rubbed the back of his neck. "How long is this going to take?"

"Forty-eight hours," Donnie replied.

"I ain't waitin' no two days!"

"That's the allotted time we give the purchaser to pay in full," Kash said.

"There's no buyer," Chevelle said point-blank.

"I see. Well, that changes things a bit." Kash stroked his chin and stood up. "I'll tell you what, Chevelle, if that is your real name. I'll give you a bit of a break. Your consignment fee is non-refundable. And the buyer's premium, you can pay."

"I thought you were going to cut me some slack?"

"I am. You get to leave today with your ride."

"I'd take the deal," Donnie blurted out.

Chevelle fumbled through his pockets. "I suppose you won't take a check."

"In God we trust. All others pay cash," Donnie smiled.

Reaching into his pocket, Chevelle produced a wad of money.

Donnie whistled. "Whew. There must be five grand there."

"You're off by a few thousand."

"You're crazy to be carrying that kind of coin around."

"I can certainly handle myself." Chevelle counted the hundred-dollar bills and handed the full amount to Kash just as a knock came at the door.

Miss Sabrina entered. "The police would like to speak to one of you."

"You know what to do." Kash eyeballed his business partner.

Donnie left the room with Miss Sabrina leading the way. As the door closed, Kash stuffed the greenbacks into his shirt pocket.

"You don't want to count it?"

"I'm sure it's all there. Just let this be a lesson to you. I don't like it when people play games at my auction."

Chevelle stuck out his hand for a shake. "No hard feelings."

He had that untrustworthy look about him as Kash reluctantly shook hands.

"How 'bout my keys."

"I'll make sure you get them right away." Reaching for the radio, Kash spoke into the mic. "Come in, Diego."

A few seconds of silence rolled past. "Go ahead," came a response.

"Chevelle would like his keys. Can you drop them off?"

"I'll leave them in his car."

"Ten-four." As Kash put down the radio he was struck with a left hook to the jaw. The blow dropped him to his knees, knocking the money out of his pocket.

"And let this be a lesson to you, big shot." Chevelle scooped up the bills, then grabbed Kash by the hair and yanked his head back. "You're not so tough after all." He followed up with a kick to the ribs.

Laying on his side, Kash took a few seconds to catch a lungful of air, then rolled onto his stomach and pushed himself back onto his feet.

Chevelle was preoccupied, consolidating his money before heading towards the door, when Kash took him by surprise, landing a punch straight to the kidneys. The blow made Chevelle gasp as he fell hard against a shelf, sending paint cans crashing to the floor. The lids flew off, splattering colors in all directions. Regaining his footing, he swung back, landing a few rabbit punches. Kash didn't flinch, instead, he countered with a blinding uppercut to the face that had the force of a freight train. The impact broke Chevelle's nose. A little winded, Kash stepped back and watched the blood spew.

76

Chevelle withdrew the Makarov pistol tucked behind his belt, and pointed it at Kash's mid-section, cocking the barrel.

"You're going to shoot me?" Kash raised his hands.

"That's the idea." Chevelle pinched the bridge of his nose to try and stop the bleeding.

"A gun like that is going to make a lot of noise in a place like this."

"Who the hell cares?"

"Well, I hope you brought enough bullets to kill all the witnesses standing outside."

Chevelle went for the door, opened it a crack, and peeked through. "This is far from over." He returned the gun to its former resting place before leaving.

Kash parked himself on the desk, rubbed his sore chin and ribs, and sighed. "Maybe I should have accepted the three million dollars."

Chapter 10

Chevelle pulled his hoodie over his head and moved swiftly through the arena. He kept his profile low, avoided eye contact, and crossed the threshold of the bidding area as Jacques signaled to have the '61 Corvette removed. Bids crested and it was time to prepare the next car for auction.

"And sold!" Jacques tapped the gavel on the lectern repeatedly before reaching for a mickey in his pocket. "At one hundred and twenty-five thousand, congratulations to bidder number three-four-three for adding one helluva automobile to your collection." He took a celebratory swig.

The new owner was in full army fatigues, as if he had just returned from duty. He stretched from his chair and acknowledged Jacques with a half salute.

Rev fired up the roadster and motored off the stage as a white '57 T-Bird took its place. He steered down a ramp and into a narrow passageway crammed with gawkers standing at the sidelines snapping photos. Tiny white flashes exploded towards Rev like spider lightning as he toured along, the spectators capturing his wry grin with every click of a shutter.

Showing off, he throttled the engine a few times, which made the exhaust resonate. A puff of smoke emitted from the tailpipe as Rev puttered onward to the parking corral.

Distracted by his pain and determined to leave discreetly, Chevelle mistakenly stepped into the path of the roadster. Rev jammed on the brakes and the car screeched to a stop. Its front bumper brushed against Chevelle's leg as he jerked, startled, and his hood flew off his head. The commotion drew unwanted attention from a small group of pedestrians.

"Ooh, that was a close call," one man said aloud.

Chevelle glared at Rev. "Watch where you're going, old man! You almost ran me down!" Feeling self-conscious he glanced at the number of faces staring at his battered appearance.

Rev rubbed his jaw and squinted as if unsure what to make of Chevelle. "Looks like someone already beat me to it." He shrugged, let out the clutch, and the motor bogged a little before pulling away.

Although he thought about shooting the loudmouth, Chevelle pulled his hood back over his head and marched on, his focus on the Vette as it turned a corner. He jogged after it in hopes that it would lead him to his beloved automobile.

Approaching an entry point to the corral, Chevelle stopped momentarily to take in the remarkable view. "Whoa," he mumbled under his breath, enamored by the array of classics parked tightly together with a Sold sign plastered across each of their windshields. For any car buff, it was like revisiting the past.

Real estate was scarce, but Rev managed to find a spot alongside Chevelle's set of wheels. He yanked up on the emergency brake and cut the engine. Rev struggled to get out from behind the steering wheel as it pressed into his gut.

Chevelle was amused watching the old fella try and leverage himself out of the low-slung sports car. It almost made him laugh, but that would have been too painful. Looking around to ensure nobody was watching, he slipped cautiously over to his tuxedo black '68 Chevelle, opened the driver's side door, climbed inside, and eased back into the seat. There, he took a second to rest. Peering into the mirror, his ego tanked. The puffy eyelids, broken nose, and dried blood smeared across his face enraged him. He wiped each spot with his sleeve as his face throbbed like a beating drum.

"Ouch. Damn it!" Frustrated, he gave up and searched for his keys, hoping they were left in the ignition, under the floor mat, or behind the sun visor, but came up empty. "Son-of-a-...."

Getting out of the car, Chevelle checked his gun for ample ammo and tucked it into the front of his pants. Wanting his keys back, he was geared up to repay Kash a visit when glancing over, he spotted some clothing resting atop the passenger seat of the '61 Vette parked next to him.

Chevelle dropped his blood-stained pullover to the ground and slipped on Kash's bomber, fedora, and gloves. He set his sights on the topless sportscar that nearly collided with him earlier and circled it like a wolf eying its prey. Attracted to its sleek lines, he traced the body's contours with his fingers, then leaped over the door and into the driver's seat. A pair of sunglasses rested on the dashboard. Chevelle tried them on. They were a perfect fit. He adjusted the rearview mirror while wondering if the car was special, perhaps belonging to a famous celebrity, like Jay Leno.

Rummaging through the glove box, he discovered a few gas receipts, a flashlight, and a package of gum. Nothing of interest, he thought, until he spotted an owner's manual and cracked open the cover. He was fanning the pages when a dated insurance slip dropped out and landed face up on his lap. The name attached was Thomas Kash.

The discovery electrified Chevelle as goosebumps popped up all over his body, creating a burst of enthusiasm that replenished his strength and lessened his aches. He was boiling over with excitement when he accidentally kneed the keys that hung from the ignition. Chevelle scoffed at the irony and basked in his sudden euphoria. With a nefarious leer, he uttered one word. "Jackpot."

Chapter 11

Donnie guided the police past the block as Rev rolled on stage in a restored white '57 T-Bird, one of the few cars remaining. As Jacques took a moment to swallow some chilled water, he gave a subtle wave as Donnie passed by with his entourage.

"The '61 Corvette was reported stolen by a Miss Sandra Kash earlier this morning," Rokeby said, glancing at his notes.

"A traffic helicopter was able to ID the vehicle just before it arrived here," Mandaumin added. "Yet, you claim the car has been registered for today's sale." He looked confused and scribbled a few handwritten notes in his pocketbook.

"I'm afraid there's been a misunderstanding," Donnie replied. "The car was a last-minute entry and has already secured a new owner. We have all the paperwork to prove it."

"We're more interested in talking to the individual who drove it here," Mandaumin said.

"I don't know who that might be, but the car is parked over there if you want to inspect it." He was pointing to the corral when he caught sight of someone dressed in Kash's attire sitting in the driver's seat.

"Thanks, but we already combed through it and found very little."

"That's odd." Donnie scratched his head. He knew Kash had been in his office speaking to Chevelle just a short while ago.

"What is?" Rokeby asked.

Donnie recognized Diego entering the corral on foot, and reached for his radio. "Diego, you read me?"

"Yup," came a voice over the airwaves.

"Who's in the '61 Vette?"

"I'll check it out," he answered back.

The Vette fired to life. Chevelle reversed, hammering the accelerator as the rear tires spun, leaving a burnout that stretched across the floor. The vehicle collided with a parked '73 Charger as the crunch of sheet metal and breaking glass echoed throughout the arena, drawing all kinds of attention.

"For Christ's sake!" Donnie blasted into his two-way radio. "We got a security breach in the corral. Suspect driving a '61 Corvette plated 'Destiny.'"

Police bolted towards the roadster.

Jacques paused the bidding from center stage. "Looks like we've got a runaway, folks. Everyone, for your safety, please remain seated."

"Soney, close all vehicle exits!" Donnie shouted into the walkie-talkie as he tried to keep pace with the officers.

Wielding his baton, Diego planted his feet firmly and stuck out his hand to beckon Chevelle to stop. As the car barreled towards him, Diego leaped above the front bumper, then slammed into the windshield with his back. The impact resonated with a thud that destroyed the glass. The baton flew out of his hand as his body bounced off the roadster and onto the floor.

The Vette veered sharply out of the corral, narrowly missing several classics as Chevelle tossed away the hat.

Diego sprang to his feet as police skirted past. Donnie stopped to check on him. "Are you alright?"

"Oddly, I feel fine." He checked his uniform for tears, but there wasn't even a scuff.

"Wait till tomorrow rolls around."

"I wanna take this guy down."

"C'mon, I know a shortcut."

The two hurdled over velvet-roped walkways and weaved through the displays, keeping the sports car in sight.

A passerby, preoccupied with his phone, stepped unknowingly into the path of the fast-moving sportscar. Chevelle swerved and lost control, careening into the eatery as patrons scrambled out of their seats. The car rampaged through a row of chairs and patio umbrellas, nearly clipping a young girl sitting at a table, sucking a milkshake through a straw. She didn't even flinch as the two-seater came to a halt next to her and stalled.

Chevelle cranked the engine, feverishly pumping the gas pedal. "C'mon, c'mon!"

Donnie and Diego were the first to come upon Chevelle.

"Let me take care of this," Diego said with assurance as Donnie hung back.

The girl sat, intrigued, eying Chevelle.

"What are you looking at?" Chevelle asked, when the motor sprang to life.

Diego charged from the side.

Chevelle whipped out his Makarov. "Don't even think about it."

Diego slid to a halt and raised his hands. Officers stormed in from behind, sidearms drawn.

"Stop! Police!" Rokeby commanded. "Drop your weapon and shut off the engine."

"Go ahead and shoot," Chevelle hollered over his shoulder. He struck a manic grin, tapping the gas pedal as the roadster spit out exhaust.

"Drop it now!" Mandaumin exclaimed.

"You want it? Come and get it!"

Diego made a run for cover.

Police kept aim and shuffled closer.

Donnie hustled over to the young girl, grabbed her hand, and hurried towards Kash, who had just arrived looking gob-smacked. The child broke loose and headed into the crowd.

Chevelle red-lined the throttle, popped the clutch, and reversed, nearly colliding with the cops as they dove out of the way. He dumped his pistol on the passenger seat, freeing up a hand to shift into first gear, leaving a wake of burning rubber, smoke and fumes.

Officers took aim and opened fire as bystanders looked for shelter. A bullet struck the Vette's taillight, another the driver's side mirror. A third buried itself in the trunk lid.

"For crying out loud! Shoot the driver, not the car!" Kash insisted.

A fourth shot took out a rear tire, and the car fishtailed. It shaved a cement pillar, spun around, and screeched to a stop, facing the opposite direction.

A few more shots continued as Chevelle ducked into the passenger seat. A slug ricocheted off the grille, another took out a headlamp, and a final shot gutted the radiator.

Chevelle punched the accelerator. The sportscar launched into a 180-degree turn and thumped past the last remaining cars waiting for the block.

"He ain't giving up," Kash said, his face in anguish as he watched sparks fly from the rim of the blown tire.

Ahead in the distance, Soney fiddled with a button that operated the last mechanically-operated bay door still open.

Donnie grabbed his radio and gave a final plea. "For God's sake, Soney, close that damn door!"

"It's stuck," Soney radioed back before abandoning his efforts. He dashed towards a glass case holding a fireman's axe mounted on the wall next to the exit. He punched through the pane, removed the weapon from its holder, and turned to face the sports car.

"He's going to be killed!" Donnie cried out.

Soney stepped to the side, swung hard, and sliced through the cable that held up the door. His force imbedded the blade into the wall as the gate came slamming down like a guillotine.

Chevelle jumped on the brakes as all four wheels locked up and squealed. A thunderous crash ensued as the car smashed into the barrier hard enough to raise the rear tires off the ground. Chevelle's body jerked violently inside the cockpit.

The crowd gasped.

Mandaumin called for backup and an ambulance.

Soney disappeared out a side entrance.

The carnage spanned the length of a soccer field. Kash darted to his hat and scooped it up. Donnie tagged alongside as they stumbled through the debris en route to the Corvette.

With guns drawn, Rokeby and Mandaumin raced towards Chevelle. As they approached the rear of the car, each moved cautiously along the sides. Kash and Donnie watched from several feet away as Chevelle lay folded on top of the steering wheel, out cold.

"Let's get him outta there," Rokeby said to Mandaumin as they pulled Chevelle out from the wreckage and placed him on the floor.

Donnie zoomed in and gave the roadster a quick assessment. The once brilliant-looking automobile was in critical condition. The sides were scored with a series of dings and dents. The back-end was buckled and rear quarters ruined. The hood was unhinged with radiator coolant steaming above a hot lifeless engine. He pulled the keys from the ignition.

"How bad is she?" Kash asked, shifting his attention away from Chevelle.

"A write-off," Donnie replied. "So, count the buyer out."

The place buzzed with chatter as spectators sought to get pictures and videos of the wreckage.

"Was it hotwired?"

"Nope." Donnie held up the keys. "Didn't have to."

Kash sighed. "I suppose it could be worse. He could have killed somebody. Or ruined my favorite hat." His voice spiked with anger as he examined his fedora and knocked off the dust.

It was the first time Donnie had ever seen Kash on the brink of a feverish outrage. "Don't lose your cool now. The media will want an interview."

"You do it. And get my jacket and gloves."

Donnie agreed with a quick nod.

Chevelle started to come around, moaning in pain.

"I hope he feels every ache for weeks," Kash said, glaring at the thief.

"I'm sure he will."

He put on his fedora and adjusted the brim. "I'll call the insurance company. In the meantime, take Destiny back to the shop."

"And do what? Mourn over it?"

"Fix it, if you can."

"What about the auction? We still got a few more cars to sell."

"I'd say the show's over." Kash turned to leave.

"What do you want me to tell the reporters?"

"Tell them our next sale will be even more exciting."

Chapter 12

Kash stretched back in his antique swivel oak chair behind a turn-of-the-century walnut desk. On an antique hall tree hung his bomber with his driving gloves sticking out of the pockets, right where Donnie had placed them.

His permanent office had all things cool—a glass-paned trophy shelf of his personal racing paraphernalia, a restored clock-face gas pump from the '30s tucked in a corner, and a wall of advertising signs that he recently acquired from a client who could not afford to pay for his car repairs. Next to his desk sat an antique safe and at the back of the room, a wet bar. The place gave him refuge, a space where he could feel at ease and plan his next move.

A ceramic mug, emblazoned with the company name, was filled with hot coffee and rested on a nickel-plated coaster. Steam swirled over the rim as Kash took a sip.

The local morning paper lay spread out in front of him, revealing the headline: "Kash and Kars Break More than Records!" A photo of the heavily damaged Corvette made the front page. The article's account of the mayhem eclipsed the many spectacular motorcars that found new adoring owners.

"It's all about sensationalism," he muttered. Filled with disappointment, Kash slid the paper to the side and stood. Hearing familiar voices outside his office, he took a few short steps to an opened window that provided a full indoor view of the restoration shop and his craftsmen at work. In the foreground, the roadster was being lowered on a hydraulic hoist.

"Nice and slow," Rev instructed. "I want to be able to reach the bolts for the rad without straining myself."

Soney played with the button, starting and stopping the lift as it jolted down an inch at a time.

"Keep it up, hero, and you'll look worse than the fool that stole this car," Rev said, threatening him with a hammer as he tried to reach across the engine.

Despite their sarcastic banter, Kash admired each of his devoted and talented crew.

Soney practically raised himself and his sibling. At 18, he and his younger brother worked at a local tire shop and saved up their money to build their own hot rod. One day, during an illegal street race, his brother fled after running down a man who had passed in front of the high-flying speedster. Soney took the rap and covered for his brother who later had a mental breakdown and died from an overdose. Sentenced for a crime he never committed, Soney remained tightlipped and did 20 years.

Over in the corner of the shop, dressed in a discolored Hawaiian shirt, Flywheel dismantled a small electric motor on a bench. A descendant of Japanese immigrants, he became an aspiring computer programmer, before spending 25 years in prison for hacking into wealthy overseas banks and transferring funds into not-for-profit accounts.

Near the back, Cosmo ground burs off the trunk lid of a '53 Cadillac. Sparks flew in different directions as he glided the tool back and forth like a painter's brush, buffing the area free of defects. He raised his tinted face shield, pushing aside salt and pepper hair to examine his work. A gifted body man, he came from good stock—his father was one of the best sheet metal bangers in the business.

Once an up-and-coming sculptor, Cosmo created a monolithic 50-foot, 40-ton piece of abstract structural art for a ritzy hotel in New York. A month after its placement, the masterpiece toppled under its own weight and destroyed the entire façade of the building, killing a mother and her child in the process. It not only ended Cosmo's career, but bought him a lengthy jail sentence.

Strolling through the center of it all was Miss Sabrina, headed towards the front office. Kash gestured with a nod as she waved to him with a brilliant white smile before disappearing through a set of doors.

Kash gravitated towards the trophy case and slid a pane across its rails, exposing his many racing awards and most cherished keepsakes. After retrieving an album that sat upright on a small marble pedestal, he went back to his desk and cracked the book open to revisit much happier times. A photo taken in 1957 featured Kash at age 12, smiling wide and resting an arm on top of a broom. It was a wonderful time to be young, innocent, and full of aspiration.

For the first few weeks of his new job, Kash swept floors, exchanged old tires for new ones, and cleaned up tools. It was nothing too exciting, except for his introductory friendship with Smokie, who had come from a long line of gifted mechanics with a hankering for being behind the wheel. His driving career came to an abrupt end when a serious crash at the Detroit Motor Speedway in '53 left him with an irreparable right leg and a bad hip. Having no other means of income, he went back to the trade.

Word had it that Smokie and Billy were, at one time, archrivals and competed at races across the country. Not long after Smokie returned to the workbench, rumor spread that the two had quietly struck a deal. While neither one would ever admit to it, one thing was clear—the decision to pair up made perfect sense. Their two strengths combined would make them virtually unstoppable. Best of all, Kash was eager to learn all they would teach him.

At the spring opener that year, Kash found himself a comfortable spot in the pits where he could watch the stock car races through his father's binoculars. About three-quarters of the way through the competition, he was momentarily distracted by an obstruction to his view.

"Hi. I'm Nikki."

Kash lowered his father's field glasses, took one look at her, stepped aside, and continued to watch the race.

"You must be Thomas."

"Yup," he said, wondering how she knew his name. She's cute though, he thought, with her dark hair, coral blue eyes, and bright smile. Even the tone in her voice is pleasant. But who is she? "What are you doing in the pits? There's no girls allowed here."

"My dad says I'm allowed."

"Oh really. And who's your father?" Kash kept his eye on the track.

"He's driving number thirty-three," Nikki said, pointing, as the pack went zooming past making a heck of a racket.

"That's Billy's car!" The binoculars nearly fell from his grip as he gave her a sidelong glance.

"Yup. That's my dad."

"How come I've never seen you before?"

"My mother doesn't like me hanging around 'grease monkeys,' so I'm supposed to watch from the stands like everybody else."

"Oh," he replied, embarrassed that his mother felt the same way about mechanics.

Nikki eyeballed the specs. "Can I see those?"

"No," he replied, pulling away. "They're very special."

"Oh, well then can you tell me how father's doing?"

"Looks like he's lagging behind a little." Kash adjusted the focus ring.

Billy was rounding the far corner, trying to stay on the inside lane to pass.

"Did you want to go and get something to eat?" she asked.

"I can't. I'm busy right now."

"I thought they hired you only to push a broom."

"What!" he said, alarmed, and glared at her.

"That's what Kyle did."

"Who's Kyle?"

"The boy father fired before you took his spot," she said, brushing hair from her face.

"I thought he just moved on."

"He did, after father fired him."

"I didn't know your dad fired anyone."

"Oh, he's fired lots of people," she said earnestly. "One time he fired the whole pit crew. Said they were nincompoops."

"*It looks like Bo Perkins, driving car number 60, is having difficulties,*" shouted the announcer over the loudspeakers as the driver sideswiped a guardrail, making a hell of a noise.

"Another time a mechanic made father lose a race," Nikki continued, uninterested in what was going on around her.

"He must've done something wrong."

"I don't think so. Father said he was just bad luck."

"So, he got rid of him?"

"He did more than that. He's never been seen again."

"Suddenly I don't feel so well." Kash rubbed his stomach.

"You're probably just hungry.

"*And Bo Perkins is definitely out of this race folks! His car is going to need some serious attention.*"

"Let me get us something. Do you have any money?" Nikki asked, smiling.

"A little. How much do you need?"

She shrugged and twirled her hair in her fingers. "How much do you have?"

Keeping an eye on the track, Kash dug in his pocket to fetch a few dollars.

"Perfect," Nikki chirped, swiping the money from his fingers.

"Hey, bring back my change."

Billy pulled closer to the front of the pack, hugging the inside lane through the turn. As he hit the straightaway there was a loud bang. The rear tires started to squeal and blue smoke billowed out from the wheel wells.

"Oh! And now it looks like Billy the Kid's in trouble!"

Kash spotted the race car dancing uncontrollably across the track.

"And there he goes!"

Billy made contact with the infield where he spun a half-dozen times before coming to a halt. He jumped out, unscathed but fuming mad, chucking his helmet and goggles to the ground.

"And they've dropped the yellow flag!"

A '57 DeSoto Fireflite convertible entered the track to caution drivers to a safer speed.

"I'm afraid the living legend won't be crossing the finish line today, folks."

Within minutes, a wrecker arrived to load the damaged stock car. By the time it was hauled to the pit for a quick review, Nikki had returned with a bag of chips and a soda. She was accompanied by a boy about the same age who was overdressed in Sunday clothes.

"Thomas, bring me that floor jack," Smokie ordered, pointing to one nearby.

Kash wheeled it over and positioned it under the rear of the vehicle. In seconds, the chassis was raised and Smokie slid beneath it. Kash crouched on all fours to get a peek at the damage.

"The rear axle snapped," Smokie said. "We'll need to take her back to the garage."

It was a narrow escape for Billy, who wandered past, temper simmering as he mumbled something in Hungarian. A few seconds later he disappeared out of the pits, not even acknowledging his daughter who stood over Kash holding snacks.

"Here you go, Thomas."

"Just set them down anywhere."

"Okay." She placed them beside her on a tool cart.

"And who are you?" the boy standing next to Nikki asked, pompously.

Kash rose to his feet, dusted himself off, smiled, and extended an arm. "I'm Thomas."

"I'm not shaking *your* dirty mitts," he said, observing Kash's filthy palms and fingernails.

Kash stuck his hands in his pockets.

"This is Dugan," Nikki said.

"Right."

She seemed uncomfortable with the awkward introduction and cut it short. "Well, we should go. I hope to see you next time." She gave Kash a coy smile before being steered away.

Kash redoubled his attention on the task at hand.

"Quite a piece of work, isn't he?" Smokie remarked from under the chassis.

"Who is that kid?"

"He's the owner's son."

"You mean Chief? The guy that owns the track?"

"Uh-huh. Now pass me an adjustable wrench."

Kash grabbed the tool on the cart and gave it to Smokie. "Why is Dugan such a turd?"

Smokie laughed. "'Cause no one's bothered to tune him up, I guess."

"I'd like to."

"Ain't worth it. If you want my advice, stay clear of him. He's bad news."

Kash reached for his snacks. He opened the soda, took a gulp, and leaned against the fender. "I don't get it. Why's Nikki hanging around him?"

"Let me tell you something, kid." Smokie slid out from under the frame, tossed the wrench aside, and peered up at him. "You think these things are high maintenance?" He tapped the door skin. "They ain't nothing compared to some women. And a girl like Nikki—when she grows up, she'll take every dollar you have."

"She already has taken every dollar."

"What do you mean?"

"I never got my change back."

Chapter 13

The glass rattled in the trophy case as engine revs from the shop shook the office walls. Kash jumped out of his chair and looked out his window.

The Vette's motor was on life support—a garden hose connected to a water pump—and Rev was pouring a stream of fuel from a soup can down the carbs, keeping the engine running on all cylinders. He was checking her over when he signaled Soney to cut the engine.

"Sometimes I think they expect me to perform miracles." Rev shook his head and tossed his hands up into the air in disgust before walking away.

It was clear that morale too had taken a downturn. Kash contemplated heading to the shop to address his team when a knock came at his door.

"Is this a bad time?" Jel asked, poking his head inside the office.

"Not at all. Come on in." Jel's arrival was a welcome distraction. Kash eagerly walked over to shake hands.

His guest gazed at all the accolades. "Are these all yours?"

Kash nodded. "Yup. All ancient history though." He grabbed the album off the desk and returned it to its former resting place.

"At least you got something to look back on."

Kash slid the glass pane closed. "Have a seat," he said, returning to his desk.

Jel stretched out in one of two black high-back leather chairs.

"I'm glad you showed up. I was hoping you'd take me up on my offer."

"To be quite honest, I hadn't given it much thought until I saw a clip of the attempted robbery on social media. It's bound to go viral."

"Regrettably, that incident got more attention than our auction results."

"How bad do you think it will be for business?"

"I keep telling myself there's no such thing as bad press, just fake news." He took a sip of his coffee. "But, I guess we'll have to wait and see if anyone sues. Here, let me show you around," he said, getting to his feet.

"Yeah, I'd like to see the place."

Strolling into the hallway, Jel took time to appreciate the many photographs on the wall depicting old race car drivers. His eyes darted from one image to the next. "You knew all these guys?"

"I raced against most of them and drank beer with the rest."

"You must have been pretty good."

"I did alright."

There was a photo of Kash winning at Daytona, trophy in hand, dated 1965. Jel stared at it with respect. "You even took home the prize, I see."

"Yeah, I got lucky a few times."

There were no photos past 1985. "Did you retire early?"

"More like the sport retired me. C'mon, I want to show you something." He threw open a set of glossy black doors designed with large, chrome-plated letters—K and K—that acted as a push bar. Inside the workshop, Kash spread out his arms like he was about to unveil a big surprise. "Here it is. The heart and soul of the operation. Over six thousand square feet of workspace and a talented crew of five that can fix, modify, or build anything you can dream up."

Jel turned in a full circle. He planted his hands on his hips and plastered a wide grin across his face. "Remarkable."

"Who's your bodyguard?" Donnie asked, upon approaching the pair.

"This is Jel Christie, the fella I've been meaning to tell you about."

"Oh."

"Donnie is the General Manager and my business partner."

"Nice to meet you." Jel wasted no time extending a hand.

"My pleasure." Donnie prepared himself for a crushing handshake. Jel didn't disappoint and gripped his hand so tightly, Donnie's knuckles popped.

"Follow me," Kash said as he continued the tour.

"We need to discuss Rev," Donnie spoke up, trailing behind, shaking off the pain.

"What's there to discuss?" Kash surveyed the ongoing work and gestured to the abandoned carcass lying on a hydraulic lift. "That's what's left of Destiny."

"Heck of a shame," Jel replied.

"Not to worry. In a few weeks, she'll be as good as new."

"He's in bad shape," Donnie said.

"Who is?" Kash glanced over his shoulder, distracted by all the activities.

"The Reverend. He ain't firing on all cylinders, so to speak."

"How's it going, Flywheel?" Kash touched him on the shoulder as he strolled past.

"Just fine." His workbench lay buried under a heap of small window regulators and power seat motors that he was busy fixing.

"Anything electrical, he's your man," Kash pointed out to Jel as they continued walking.

"He's starting to lose it," Donnie said in a raised voice as the work area got noisier. "I'm tellin' ya, he's gotta go,"

"You still rambling on about Rev?"

"Yeah. His memory ain't good, and his hands shake like he's battling withdrawals. We need to cut him loose," Donnie replied point-blank.

"Can't do that."

"Why not?"

"Without us, he wouldn't make it a week."

Jel's face twisted as he spotted a '48 Tucker in the corner, its trunk open. "Is that a—"

"Yes, it is. I bought one just like it back in the seventies. I paid six thousand dollars for it, then sold it a few years later for twenty-five thousand. Thought I had made a killing. Today, it's worth well over a million." He moseyed across the floor to a '53 Cadillac being prepped for paint. Jel and Donnie followed.

Diligently masking an area to protect it from overspray, Cosmo, dressed in solid white coveralls with only his face exposed, went about his business. His workmanship was impeccable.

"Will I be able to see your million-dollar smile in its reflection when it's done?" Kash asked.

"No question about it." Cosmo smiled, revealing his two missing front teeth.

Pulling Jel aside for a brief one-on-one, Kash spoke into his ear. "He's the best paint and body guy in the state. But don't tell him that or else he'll want a raise."

Donnie poked Kash in the arm. "You need to talk to him right away if you want to meet the deadline for the next sale."

"Alright, fine." Kash glanced around, but the preacher was nowhere in sight. "Where did Friar Tuck disappear to?"

"Outside." Donnie pointed.

"He's probably just having a bad day."

"Every day is a bad day for him," Donnie replied before they marched through an open bay door.

The weather was a sunny 78-degrees Fahrenheit as the trio stepped into the fresh air. Stretched halfway across the fender of a two-tone white and blue '58 Merc, Rev, with his sleeves rolled up, fiddled with a matching set of tri-power carburetors. The engine groaned deeply as Soney sat behind the wheel riding the throttle.

"Keep your foot off the gas until I say so," Rev hollered, as he tried to adjust the idle. He fumbled with a flathead screwdriver.

Kash pulled alongside to bring him some cheer. "How's the Holy Roller this morning?"

"Ready for the boneyard." He rested his tool on the intake manifold.

"What seems to be the problem?"

"These carbs need a rebuild. They're over sixty years old for Christ's sake."

Jel whistled admirably at the mammoth classic. "That's the prettiest girl I've ever seen."

"Who the hell's this?" Rev asked, pulling away from the engine to size up the newcomer.

"Rev, this is—" Donnie began.

"Never mind, I ain't got time for introductions. I got a whole list of crap to fix."

Ogling the portly beast of a vehicle, Jel couldn't keep his excitement to himself. "Man, I can't believe my eyes. A Super Marauder! Do you know how few of these exist?"

"Yup. Only a small handful," Kash said.

"Some consider this to be the first true muscle car." Jel walked around the coupe with his jaw on the floor. "Continental kit, dual exhaust, Breezeway window option, jukebox interior, wraparound windshield—man, she's got everything you could want in a luxury automobile."

"I forgot you like the full-sized models," Kash replied.

Jel drifted back to the front end where he drooled over all the hi-performance goodies. "And this is it. The Mack Daddy of all displacements. The 430 cubic-inch big-block jacked with a whopping 10.5-to-1 compression. You're talking 400 horses tied to a push-button automatic." He beamed like a kid drawing a prize out of his first Happy Meal.

"Yup, she'll pass everything except a gas station," Rev said. "By the way, keep your hands off the merchandise. You're leaving prints everywhere." He tossed over a clean shop towel that had been sitting on the cowl.

"Sorry, couldn't help myself," Jel replied, wiping where he touched the beautiful vehicle.

"You seem to know a thing or two about cars," Donnie said.

"He's an old school mechanic," Kash offered up. "And I'm sure a darn good one."

Rev caught wind of the conversation and rolled his eyes.

"Those are factory Holley 2300 carburetors still with their original ID tags," Jel said.

"So they are," Rev replied rather gruffly, while glaring at Jel.

"They're a bit tricky to setup."

"Try damn near impossible." Sweat dripped from Rev's forehead.

"Mind if I take a look?"

Rev's face contorted with resentment and frustration. "As a matter of fact—."

"Take it easy Rev," Kash said calmly. "Let Jel take a crack at it. Just for the heck of it."

"Fine. Knock yourself out." He stepped back and let the big fella pass.

"Thanks."

"Uh-huh," Rev mumbled in resentment, arms folded.

Huddling close to the engine, Jel picked up the screwdriver and began tweaking the idle screw on each carb. The engine soon slowed and fell into a melodic rhythm. "There, that outta do it." He pulled himself away, appearing confident to have remedied the problem.

"Sounds pretty good to me," Kash replied.

"It's music to my ears," Donnie added, looking over the motor as it hummed along.

It was a devastating blow for Rev as he stood in awe. He leaned in to take a closer look at the tunings, and scratched his head. "Beginners luck."

"Shut her off," Kash shouted as Soney cut the engine.

"Nice work," Donnie said.

"Look, I could use another mechanic," Kash stated as he watched Rev's jaw drop. "Even if it's just temporary, and I will pay you the same rate as your fellow tradesmen."

"I'm good with that."

"There's just one thing I need to know," Donnie said. "What'd you go to prison for?"

"Stealing high-end sports cars. Lamborghini, Ferrari, Porsche, anything that ran hi-octane."

"Since when did you like the fast ones?" Kash asked.

"In my youth."

"Were you running a chop shop?" Donnie asked with concern.

"No, that'd be sacrilege. I exported to offshore buyers who had very deep pockets."

"Sounds like you made a lot of money," Kash said.

"I did, until I got busted."

"We have some pretty strict ground rules with zero tolerance," Donnie said with gravity. "No fighting, drinking, or foul language. Well, with the exception of Rev as he's a lost cause."

"The hell you say!" Rev barked, overhearing them.

"I can live with that. I'm just grateful for the opportunity."

"I know you won't let me down." Kash patted him on the shoulder.

"When do you want me to start?" Jel asked, eagerly.

"Right away if you can."

"Now, just what in Sam Hill's going on here?" Rev bellowed from the sidelines. "Am I getting turfed? Set out to pasture like some swayback mule." He gathered up his tools like he was getting ready to walk off the job.

"You? You're irreplaceable," Kash said with assurance. "But you just got someone to help share the load."

"Hogwash. It's about replacing the old with the new." He wandered off inside, muttering to himself.

"Never mind him. He'll get over it." Kash said, realizing he should have handled the situation more tactfully. "But before we put you to work on that Tucker engine, we'll need to find a pair of overalls large enough to fit you."

"Easier said than done," Donnie said. Jel responded with an unenthused brow lift that was interrupted by a short ringing bell.

"What's that noise?"

"Lunch," Donnie replied.

"I didn't bring any," Jel said.

"Don't worry. Today, it's on me," Kash responded.

Chapter 14

It was the summer of 1961 and a late afternoon sun fell upon the Mount Clemens racetrack. The crew had just wrapped up a long day of practice runs with an unforgettable 16th birthday surprise for Kash: a blue and white racing suit—a spot-on match to Billy's. There could not have been a greater gift, or so Kash thought.

He slipped away to dress up in his new attire and returned to show it off. Smokie took a few snapshots with his Brownie camera as Kash stood proudly next to a '61 Cooper T-54 finished in cobalt blue with a helmet and goggles held tightly by his side.

Nikki stepped forward from the group to make her presence known.

"Hey, you made it!" Kash exclaimed.

"Of course. How could I miss your birthday?" She kissed him on the cheek, then handed him an envelope.

He pulled out a birthday card and flipped it open. Inside were the hand-written words: *To the one I love. Happy 16th Birthday Thomas.* The message brought a smile to his face as he gazed at Nikki with deep affection.

Before he could say a word, he was pulled outside by the crew to where an old clunker rested—a '51 Hudson Hornet that had a few less dings than a derby car.

"Hop in and get behind the wheel," Smokie urged.

"What? In this wreck?" He was hoping to have a crack at the sporty Indy car.

"Did you think you were going to drive the Cooper?"

"Well, no, I mean, I guess not." He gave the Hudson a second look. It didn't resemble a trophy winner at all. It had been painted over in brown primer, and all its chrome badging, including the hood ornament, were long gone. The front bumper and grill were completely bent out of shape, and the sides were scored as if the vehicle had been severely sideswiped. "Is it safe?"

"Safe?" Smokie sounded offended. "I'll have you know this car won at Daytona ten years ago." He performed a short drum roll on the rooftop that ended with a whack. The vibration shook loose a mouse nest which then fell from the headliner. "She's tired and beat up, but dependable."

Kash hoisted himself through the side window and into the cockpit. "Smells awful." He slid on his helmet and goggles as the crew pushed the car onto the track for some last-minute pictures.

Billy approached and placed a hand on his shoulder. "You have learned a great deal about the mechanics of these machines, young Thomas, but what I cannot teach you is the feel of the car. Each one behaves a little differently. You must learn that for yourself if you are to progress."

Buckling himself in, Kash took note of his surroundings. The steering wheel, black with grit, felt gross. A few gauges were missing from the dashboard, and a spring sticking out from the seat continuously prodded his butt.

"Just treat her like a lady on a first date." Billy delivered a wink.

"I'll be gentle, alright. Otherwise, she might fall apart." He tightened the strap under his chin.

"Fire it up!" Billy commanded as he slapped the roof and more debris fell from the inside, soiling the driver.

After brushing himself off, Kash turned over the engine and it sparked to life with hesitation. It sounded mean, despite needing a tune-up. Kash kept one foot riding the gas as the motor misfired and nearly stalled. Each shake and rattle made him contemplate driving it to the scrapyard. It was a heap, but through some miracle, it ran.

A quick check of the instruments showed that the oil pressure and amps were good. Fuel was less than half a tank. He revved the engine twice and puffs of blue smoke belted out the back, enough to create a diversion for a getaway.

Kash shifted into gear and aimed for the track. The crew jogged alongside for a few steps before he throttled down to feed the thirsty twin carburetors, bracing himself for the neck-snapping torque that never came from the tired straight-six.

After the first few laps, his confidence got the better of him. A stream of black soot emanated out the straight pipes as he hunkered down on the accelerator on a straightaway. Entering a corner, he lost control and spun into the infield, unscathed in a cloud of dust. Coughing and gagging with a mouthful of grit, he waited for the view to clear.

In the distance, he saw the crew jumping and waving for him to carry on, but Kash needed no further motivation. Unshaken by the minor incident, he kicked the throttle down and the rear tires trenched a path. In a matter of seconds, the formerly defiant race car fishtailed onto the dirt track with its handler eager to burn off the remaining carbon trapped in the bowels of the engine.

A few laps later, he seemed to have the hang of it and maintained tight control despite a less-than-satisfactory speed. It was an adventure like no other. The adrenaline rush was extreme, causing the hair on his arms to stand erect—a sensation he never experienced before in his life.

There would be no plans to end the date early, and a thought did cross his mind about running the old girl to empty before calling it quits.

Kash had been bitten by the racing bug. His fate was sealed and his mind obsessed with becoming the next great race car driver, following on the heels of his idol, Billy the Kid.

Chapter 15

Tom Sr. entered the grounds unnoticed. He immediately spotted the crew fixated on the Hudson as it circled the track. With every lap the vehicle increased speed. On the next pass, it sailed around a corner fast enough to slingshot into the straightaway. Smokie withdrew a stopwatch from his jacket and hit the start button. The crew cheered on in celebration.

"Hello gentlemen," Tom said, making his appearance known.

"You're early," Smokie replied, nervously. He glanced at his watch, then reached into his pocket for a smoke.

"I figured I'd surprise the birthday boy and take him out for ice cream." Tom caught a glimpse of the battered race car. "What's Billy doing driving that old relic?"

No one said a word.

"Looks like he's taking it slower than usual. Are there mechanical problems?"

Smokie choked as he inhaled his freshly lit cig. He glanced at Billy, who stood several feet away.

"She's running fine," Billy said. He remained focused on the track.

"Oh, I didn't even notice you standing there."

"Didn't see me, or didn't expect me?"

"Actually both. What's going on?"

"I'm getting a first-hand look at what the future may hold."

Tom brought his binoculars up to his eyes to get a closer look at the person behind the wheel. The crew stood tensed.

"I really need to clean these. Can barely see anything." Tom removed a cloth from his shirt to polish up the lenses.

Billy raised an eyebrow as the car zipped past at a steady 65 mph. A cloud of dust covered every onlooker as Smokie confirmed the time. He glanced over to his teammates and gave a thumbs up.

"Your man seems to be picking up the pace," Tom added.

The crew chuckled, but Tom couldn't figure out what was so funny.

"He's doing better than expected," Billy said.

"Where is Thomas, by the way?"

"Right where he belongs."

"Sorry?"

Billy turned to face him. "He's having his cake and eating it too."

Tom stared on, perplexed.

"Look for yourself," Billy said as he pointed to the Hudson with his index finger.

"You got to be kidding me." Tom dropped the cloth and hoisted the binoculars up to his eyes so fast he bumped his brows. "He doesn't even hold a learner's permit." Adjusting the focus ring, he got an up-close visual of his son.

"He's a born natural," Billy replied.

"I can't believe it. If his mother knew this, she'd have a cow."

"Then I suggest you don't tell her."

Tom winced at the idea. The crew dropped their heads, a sad attempt at hiding their amusement.

"Do you want me to wave him in?"

Tom fell silent and deliberated. "No, let him do a few more laps first."

Billy chuckled and delivered a decisive nod.

"Although, I think it's best I watch from a distance. It might take him off his game if he knew I was watching."

"Good idea. I think we should all step back." Billy motioned to his crew.

By the 10th lap, Kash soared past at an estimated 70 mph. It was clear that he had every intention of edging the race car to higher speeds. Billy, seemingly convinced his young trainee might be pressing his luck a bit too much, gave Smokie a go-ahead to signal him in.

When he saw the black flag raised, Kash reluctantly exited the course and rolled into the pits. His team hailed him as if they had just witnessed his first victory race. He rolled to a stop, cut the engine, and pulled himself out as his peers rushed to his side to give him a hand. With his feet on the ground, he removed his safety gear and tossed it on the seat.

"Well kid, you looked great out there." Smokie threw Kash a torn cloth to wipe his face.

"Why'd you call me in? I still had a quarter of a tank left." He rubbed the rag over his cheeks and forehead as Nikki grabbed his hand and locked fingers.

"That's enough excitement for one day," Billy said.

"I was just getting warmed up." His enthusiasm had peaked. "When can I go again?"

"In due time. Now let's get these wheels back inside and call it a day."

The crew scrambled on Billy's orders and pushed the vehicle towards the garage when Tom advanced towards his son.

"I'll see you soon." Nikki gleamed at Kash before leaving his side. She waved to Tom who acknowledge her with a nod.

"I like the outfit," Tom said.

"Thanks. It's a gift from the team."

"Let's go for a walk." Tom gestured towards the grounds as he strolled alongside his son.

"How long have you been here?" Kash asked.

"Long enough to watch you circle a few times."

"You angry about it?"

Tom shook his head while keeping pace. "There ain't much use in getting upset. Sooner or later, you'll be back out there again doing what you love."

"I suppose you're right."

"I am."

"What are you thinking?"

"Truthfully?"

"Yeah."

"I might be looking at the next Billy the Kid."

"Now I know you're blowing smoke up my tailpipe."

Tom chuckled. "No. Son, I'm telling you to aim high."

"That's a pretty tall order, dad."

"Trust me, don't set your goals too low. You'll be disappointed."

"I don't know. I've got a long, hard road ahead of me."

"Yes, you do, but you've been dreaming about this your whole life, haven't ya?"

"That I have."

"Then, when the time is right, you gotta make the jump with both feet."

They reached the grandstands and rested.

"How do I prepare myself for that?" Kash took a seat.

His father put a leg up next to him. "Through hard work, focus, and believing in yourself."

"Why are you telling me this?"

"Because I want you to succeed, be the best *you* can be, and go as far as *you* can. And no matter what, don't let anyone kill your dreams. You understand?"

"Yes, sir. But I do need practice." Kash gazed out towards the track.

"That'll come, and you've got a whole crew to help get you there."

"You got this all figured out, don't you?"

"I wish I did. I only know one thing."

"What's that?"

"That you have unlimited potential."

Daylight faded and the temperature began to drop. A subtle, cool breeze floated in, producing a chill in the air.

"C'mon, we should be heading home." He tapped his son's leg. "Your mother probably has dinner already waiting."

Kash remained still, closed his eyes, and meditated.

"What are you doing?"

"I'm dreaming about heading towards the finish line. I can see the crowd going wild, jumping out of their seats as the checkered flag is about to drop."

"You're forgetting one thing."

"What's that?" Kash asked, before he opened his eyes.

"A driver's license." His father laughed.

Chapter 16

I nside the restoration shop, near a large open area, two sawhorses and a sheet of plywood made for a makeshift table. Donnie tossed a linen sheet ridden with holes overtop as Soney arranged the folding chairs.

Merrily whistling away, Flywheel was dispersing paper plates, plastic utensils, and paper napkins when Miss Sabrina barreled through the double doors, struggling to manage the remaining bags of takeout.

Jel rushed to her aid and hoisted the contents onto the table. "Smells good," he said, taking a whiff.

"Eat like you're at home, just not as much," Kash teased. His comment raised a smile as Jel removed the items from each bag and cracked open the lids.

The aroma of Asian cuisine drifted across the room.

"What's the occasion?" Jel took a seat, placed a napkin on his lap, and waited for everyone to get settled.

"Kash celebrates with a meal after every auction. It's his way of showing his appreciation for our hard work." Donnie loosened his collar.

"Well, I'm honored," Jel said.

Cosmo steadied a large pitcher of fresh lemonade. Before sitting down, he poured eight glasses without spilling a drop.

Moving sluggishly, and last to arrive, Rev took a seat at the end of the table, opposite Jel. Sweat ran down the side of his face.

"Are you okay?" Miss Sabrina asked, concerned, as she placed a glass of the sweet stuff in front of Rev. "You don't look so well."

"I'm about to get canned," Rev growled, huffing along with a discontented pout. He belted down the drink, then belched. "Top me off, if you don't mind."

Miss Sabrina obliged with a refill as Rev pulled out a few antacid tablets and swallowed them down with his drink. He pulled out a handkerchief and blew his nose, failing to realize his colleagues were expecting him to say grace.

"While we're waiting, I'd like to introduce Jel Christie to the team," Kash said. "He's a mechanic by trade and will be working alongside Rev."

"Jel. Is that short for Jalopy?" Rev asked.

"It's short for Jelani," Jel replied.

"Could have fooled me."

"We could use the extra help," Donnie said putting in order his fork, knife, and spoon.

"Use the help, my ass!" Rev stabbed an eggroll with his fork.

"Aren't you going to say grace?" Miss Sabrina reached out and touched his arm.

Rev glanced at all the faces staring back at him. "If you insist. But for the record, I don't feel we need another mechanic."

"You should be thankful," Kash said.

"Why the hell should I?"

"Because you've been pushing yourself pretty hard." Kash picked up the container of fried rice and scooped some onto his plate.

Rev narrowed his eyes at Donnie. "Thanks for killing my overtime."

Donnie's face twisted into a grimace.

"There'll be lots of overtime coming," Kash said. "We got another auction coming up fast and we're short on time."

"And money," Donnie added.

Not wanting to alarm his crew about the company's financial crisis, Kash nudged Donnie under the table.

"Well, who interviewed Jalopy?"

Kash rolled his eyes, knowing the nickname was sure to stick.

"His name is Jel," Miss Sabrina said, respectfully.

Kash aimed his thumb at himself. "I did."

Rev snorted in disgust. "Why the hell didn't anyone ask me about this?"

"I wanted to make it a surprise."

"It's a surprise alright. Like a sucker punch. How do we know he's any good?"

"For crying out loud," Donnie blurted out. "He just diagnosed the '58 Merc in a matter of seconds, while you fiddled for the past hour."

"He got lucky." Rev's face turned red.

"Oh really?"

"This job involves a lot more than just being able to swing a wrench or turn a screwdriver. You gotta have mitts like a surgeon." He displayed his crooked fingers, dirty fingernails, and numerous scrapes, cuts, and bruises. Rev quickly withdrew them from view. "And a mind that is sharp and in constant perpetual motion with the natural vibrations of the mechanical universe."

"Natural vibrations of the mechanical universe." Donnie gawked at Kash. "He's been drinking again."

Miss Sabrina shushed Donnie.

Leaning forward in his seat, Rev laid down the most essential, philosophical piece of knowledge for all car gurus. "The engine you see, is the very soul of the automobile. Without it, the body is just, well, stillborn."

"That's deep," Flywheel said.

"I don't think I ever heard it explained that way." Miss Sabrina looked confused.

"Ah, not to worry, Rev. Jel's the right man for the job," Kash said.

"Yeah, but does he know anything about the auction business?"

"About as much as you did when you started here." Donnie dipped his spoon into his wonton soup and gave it a stir.

"He has a point there," Cosmo said.

"Nobody asked you." Rev reached for a chicken ball using his bare hand while Miss Sabrina wasn't looking, and took a bite and munched away. "What I mean is, can he think on his feet?"

"I believe so." Kash winked at Jel.

"'Cause in this job you wear more than one hat. It's vital that his understanding of the classics span beyond mechanical principles."

"What are you getting at?" Donnie asked.

"It's about knowing your damn history!" Rev exclaimed. He pounded his fist on the table, bouncing the utensils. "You can't know a car unless you know its documented past, just like you can't fully appreciate a person without being told their life experiences."

"Interesting analogy," Flywheel replied. "I'm impressed."

"I suggest we give him a test," Rev said.

"Uh-oh, here it comes, a pissing contest," Cosmo said.

"Jel already passed the interview." Kash took a swig of lemonade.

"That's okay," Jel replied. "If it'll help calm matters, I'll play along."

"You don't have to," Donnie said.

"It's alright. I got this."

Kash rested back in his chair, sighed, and shrugged his shoulders. "Alright, suit yourself."

"See what's left of that Corvette over there?" Rev asked as he pointed to the lift holding Destiny.

Jel nodded.

"How many of those were produced back in '61?"

Jel rubbed his shaved head and gazed at the ceiling.

 Rev grimaced. "Well, how many?"

"I believe 14,531."

Rev remained straight-faced.

"Is that correct?" Cosmo asked.

"Yes, it is," Kash said, rather surprised.

Rev fired back. "Wheelbase."

"102 inches," Jel replied.

"What about drive train options?"

Jel counted on his fingers. "Three-speed manual, four-speed manual, automatic, including dual four-barrel carbs, or if you had the money—fuel injection."

"Simply amazing," Donnie said in near disbelief. He folded his arms and leaned back to study the situation.

"What was the exterior color of every eleventh Mustang that rolled off the line in 1965?"

"Rangoon Red."

"Holy crap," Miss Sabrina blurted out before covering her mouth.

"No one has ever been able to answer every question correctly," Flywheel said.

"How do you know so much about automobiles?" Donnie asked.

"I learned to read from car magazines. Only thing that could hold my attention."

"Okay hotshot, how many of those Tucker automobiles were produced?" He pointed to the one under repair.

"Look out, Jel. He's shifted into second gear," Cosmo said, reaching for the steamed vegetable platter before getting his wrist slapped by Miss Sabrina.

"We haven't said grace yet," she said.

"Fifty-one, including the Tin Goose prototype," Jel responded without hesitation.

"Engine?" Rev asked in anger.

"Prototype or production?" Jel asked, quenching his thirst.

"Both," Rev said, angered.

"Whoa," the remaining team members said in unison as they watched the battle unfold.

"The Tucker 589 cubic-inch engine was the prototype. Production was a six-cylinder ALV 335, helicopter motor retrofitted to the car."

"Gettin' tired Rev?" Donnie asked.

"No, just getting *revved* up." He grinded his teeth. "The Ferrari V12."

"Look out, Jel. He's skipped third and dropped her right into fourth gear," Cosmo said.

"Obviously having no luck with the American cars, he's moved on to foreign makes," Flywheel scoffed.

"What about it?" Jel asked.

"What's the first model produced?" Rev's face turned beet red with fierce determination.

Jel paused for a second. "That was the Ferrari 125 Sport. Debuted on May 11, 1947."

The room broke out into applause. Rev appeared exasperated.

"Wow!" Miss Sabrina gasped.

"Outstanding job." Donnie patted Jel on the shoulder before addressing Rev. "It's time you admit your defeat, and say grace."

"Not so fast." Rev licked his lips. "I ain't done yet."

"But the food's getting cold," Cosmo said with disappointment, hovering his hand an inch over the plate of beef chow mein.

"Touch that grub and I'll throttle ya!" Rev growled.

"Easy, no need to get hostile," Cosmo replied.

"I'm gonna say the name of the manufacturer and you tell me what the letters stand for."

"What?" Jel asked, perplexed.

"That has no bearing on anything," Donnie said.

"And I say it does!" Rev bellowed. "If he's gonna work with me, he's got to know his stuff."

"He already knows his stuff," Kash said.

"Yes, I feel Jel has more than proven himself to all of us," Flywheel said with confidence.

"I didn't ask for your opinion," Rev said.

"So what gear is this?" Jel asked.

"Overdrive," Rev replied with authority. "Tell me what does IVECO, stand for?"

"Never heard of it," Miss Sabrina said, pondering.

"Industrial Vehicle Corporation," Jel said.

"BMW."

"That's easy, Bayerische Motoren Werke," Jel replied in his best German accent.

"Again, incredible," Flywheel replied.

"Fiat."

"Fabrica Italiano Automobilica Torino," he stated with an Italian inflection.

"You mean it's not 'Fix It Again, Tony?'" Cosmo joked.

Donnie shook his head.

"Got anything else?" Kash asked.

Rev slumped back in his chair. "Just one," he said, perspiring heavily. Rev dragged his drink across his forehead, then sat it back down and began to rub his neck and arms, as if in distress. "Pontiac."

"*Pontiac*." For the first time, Jel appeared stumped.

"There is no meaning behind the name Pontiac," Donnie said.

"Sure there is." Rev pointed like a drill sergeant.

"Pontiac was Obwandiyag." Soney gestured with a nod. "A great Odawa war chief."

"Oh boy," Kash muttered, sensing trouble.

"It's a trick question," Miss Sabrina said. "The letters must stand for something else." She took out a pen and began to scribble out the letters on her napkin in hopes of solving the riddle.

"Pontiac," Jel repeated under his breath.

"That's right, Pontiac," Rev said. "So, what is it, Jalopy?" He stared piercingly at him.

A moment of silence gave the impression that Rev may have outfoxed his opponent. Then, Jel spoke with humility.

"I think I got it figured out. 'Poor Ole Negro Thinks It's A Cadillac.'"

Donnie choked on a gulp of lemonade as the room fell still.

"Oh my," Miss Sabrina gasped. "I *never* would have got that."

Rev contemplated a suitable response. "It's 'Poor Ole Native Thinks It's A Cadillac,' not 'negro.' But I guess it could go either way." He started to laugh and slapped his knee as Soney gave him the stink eye.

"I hope you're satisfied," Donnie said steaming mad.

"What? It's a joke." He shrugged it off.

"I think we should maybe skip grace and just start eating," Cosmo suggested.

"I agree." Flywheel reached for a container of breaded chicken with gravy and helped himself.

"Well some of us might not have found it very funny," Donnie replied.

"Oh, c'mon." Rev had a smile as big as a peach and a sparkle in his eye. "Can I help it if the world's gone too politically correct?"

"If there's something you want to say, we can discuss it in my office," Kash offered.

"I ain't got anything to say."

"Except grace." Miss Sabrina put her palms together.

"I think that would be wise," Donnie said, staring coldly at Rev.

"Fine," he snapped, tucking a napkin inside the top of his collar. "Since this might be my last meal here, I should say a prayer."

"Bow your heads," Kash ordered.

While he thought no one was looking, Rev pulled out a flask. He unscrewed the top, took a swig, and emptied the remainder into his glass. He tucked the decanter back into his pocket.

"Anytime you're ready," Kash said, disappointed by what he saw.

Rev rested his elbows firmly on the table, fingers interlocked. He cleared the phlegm from his throat and started a prayer. "Bless us, O Lord, and these, Thy gifts, which we are about to receive from Thy bounty. Through Christ, our Lord. Amen."

"Amen," the team repeated.

While the grub was being passed around, Kash leaned over to speak to Jel. "Thanks for being a good sport."

"No worries. Although I can't say the same for that gentleman sitting over there," he said, gesturing towards Soney, who appeared perturbed.

"Ah, that's his usual expression."

"Oh."

"You'll have to excuse Rev," Donnie said as he joined the conversation. "He's been more disgruntled than usual."

"I don't think he likes me," Jel replied, half-joking as he helped circulate a dish being passed from one person to another.

"For the record, he doesn't like anybody," Donnie added.

"Though I can't say I've ever seen him that sour." Kash twiddled with his fork while observing Rev guzzle his beverage. "Something's definitely not right."

Donnie took another spoonful before dragging a serviette across his lips. "I've been trying to tell you that, but you don't listen."

There wasn't much on Rev's plate as he seemed to zone out. A few seconds later he snapped out of it, withdrew a piece of folded paper, unraveled it, and smoothed out the edges so he could write on it.

"You're too easy on him," Donnie said. "I would have kicked him to the curb for his shenanigans a long time ago."

"I know." Kash sighed. "But he's got nobody but us." He paused to think about the other possible reasons for his teammate's bad behavior. "Perhaps if we knew his entire life's story, we'd be just as troubled."

"That's a good point," Jel said. "You never know how fragile he might be."

"I know if you can break through that gruff exterior, there's a heart of gold inside," Kash said.

"Yeah, it's encased in concrete," Donnie replied.

"Is he really a preacher?" Jel asked.

"Nonpracticing." Kash reached for some bean sprouts.

"He's an ex-televangelist," Donnie commented as he tipped his bowl up and downed the soup.

"What happened to him?"

"No one really knows for sure. I'm guessing embezzlement, fraud, or prostitution." Donnie sampled the steamed mixed vegetables. "Or maybe all three."

"That's unfortunate."

"You fellas enjoying your conversation over there?" Rev asked. The remark caught the entire crew's attention and the room fell quiet. "I can hear you rambling on about me." He stared at the trio. "You wanna know my life's story?"

"No, we're good, thanks," Donnie said.

"It just so happens I have it all written down right here in front of me."

"Are you serious?" Miss Sabrina, interested, pulled the sheet of paper towards her. "It's a poem. How beautiful."

"I find it therapeutic."

"So are ballet lessons, I'm sure." Cosmo chortled.

A roar of laughter erupted from everyone at the table, except Rev and Miss Sabrina.

"Don't pay any attention to them," she said. "What's your poem about?"

"I told you. It's my life story." Rev scribbled down a few more lines on the paper. "Do you want to hear it?"

The facial expressions of Donnie, Soney, Cosmo, and Flywheel said it all. Whatever remarks come out of Rev's mouth next will surely offend someone, Kash thought.

"I think we've heard enough outta you for one day," Donnie said.

"Oh, c'mon," Miss Sabrina replied. "This is a great opportunity for Rev to share something very personal." She rubbed his arm. "I never took you for a poet."

"Actually, this is my first draft."

"How wonderful," Miss Sabrina replied. "Well, we're all ears."

"Rev," Kash said in a calm voice. "Why don't you just eat your food?"

"'Cause I ain't hungry." He pushed his plate aside.

"Alright then." Kash put down his fork and tossed his napkin off his lap. "I'm gonna ask everyone to pause for a minute while Rev takes the floor."

"You really think this is a good idea?" Donnie asked.

Rev appeared glossy-eyed. The alcohol had kicked in. The odds of him insulting someone had just gone up.

"What can I do? He claims it's therapy." Kash flung his arms in the air as Rev pulled out a pair of reading glasses, cleared his throat repeatedly, then read aloud.

Thank you dear Lord
For Bugatti and Cord,
Two of my favorite makes.

As a young man I knew,
What was in me to do,
So excited, I'd get the shakes.

I loved cars so much,
I became a mechanic as such,
So I could work on them
Twenty-four-seven.

Now there's a lot to be said,
For taking your dreams to bed,
And I felt I had made it to heaven.

Cosmo nodded in agreement.

Yes, I worked day and night,
And did everything right,
To the top of the mountain
I'd reached.

Then I found my wife in bed,
With both Harry and Fred,
Well, our marriage had certainly been breached.

Donnie shook his head in disbelief. Kash squinted painfully.

So, I hit the road in my hot rod,
Where I unexpectedly found God,
And headed to church in cheer.

There I hung up my wrench,
Sat down on a bench,
And began to lend an ear.

I was taught Proverbs and grace,
And to put a smile on my face,
Whenever life had me beaten down.

Rev cracked a smile that was almost comical.

I sought glory in what's right,
No more drinkin' and bar fights,

I became a man of worship in that town.

Ten years went by,
In the blink of an eye,
And I was called Reverend, Father, or Friar.

Then along came sweet Betty,
One look and I turned sweaty,
If I said any different, I'd be a liar.

Yup she was wild and fun,
And, well, son-of-a-gun,
I found myself led into temptation.

"Here we go," Donnie whispered under his breath as he hung his head.

A drinker and gambler,
We made love in my Rambler,
Where I worked off my frustration.

Now it may sound somewhat corny,
But I was pretty horny,
And it didn't take long for rumors to start.

Cosmo sat spellbound and Flywheel raised an eyebrow. Jel appeared gobsmacked while Soney and Miss Sabrina scanned the floor like something had just rolled off the table.

Unlike Auburn and Ace,
I was deemed a disgrace,
Soon after, it all fell apart.

Fast women and wine,
Will make your heart red-line,
And keep your wallet dry.

While I still have the Lord,
And my hot roddin' Ford,
I think of those days gone by.

Now I've been told that I'm bitter,
Since my life went down the shitter,
But I am the one who's to blame.

As I sit within these walls,
After being kicked in the balls,
It's clear I've reached the end of my game.

I'm way past my prime,
And don't have much time,
So Jel, you go work on that Tucker.

Since you have my job,
'Cause I'm just an old, angry slob,
I say, good luck to you, mother—.

"Rev!" Kash shouted and stared him down. "Enough! I'm sending you home to cool off."

"Fine by me!" He threw down his napkin and shot out of his chair like something bit him on the rear end. Rev wobbled. "Whoa." He rested one hand on the table, the other over his chest as if something had a hold on him.

"What's wrong?" Miss Sabrina asked, panic stricken.

The crew rose to their feet as Rev leaned forward and moaned. He didn't say a word, but his body swayed like he had been on the high seas. Then again, maybe it was the booze.

"He doesn't look so well," Flywheel said, appearing concerned.

"I think he just stood up too fast." Cosmo went to fetch the chair that got kicked out when Rev jumped to his feet, but it was too late. Gripping the table covering in one hand, Rev keeled backward and pulled the entire afternoon meal and drinks to the floor.

Miss Sabrina screamed as Rev crashed onto his back with a dull thud.

The crew rushed to his side as Donnie turned sharply towards Kash. "I think he's having a heart attack!"

Chapter 17

It was the spring of 1964 and Kash raced around the Mount Clemens track with his fenderless '32 Ford flathead V8 roadster as the sun bounced off the glorious aluminum-dressed engine exposed at the sides.

Billy watched through a pair of binoculars from a conference room window high atop the stadium. He had just returned from a funeral, where Chief was laid to rest, and was still wearing his light gray suit and dress shoes from that morning. In the same room sat Dugan, dressed all in black with slicked-back hair. He looked like a gangster.

Dugan's lawyer, an elderly gentleman with a bad comb-over, sat beside him in faded attire. One thick legal document was neatly placed on the table, ready for Billy's signature. The two waited impatiently.

Billy adjusted the focus on his eyepiece while glued to the action. Kash seemed like he was in his element, wearing a plain white T-shirt, jeans, and sunglasses. In the passenger seat sat his beloved Nikki. She was stunning in her black slacks and silver-colored top, holding the brim of her white hat as the Deuce barreled around the dirt course. On every bend, Kash pushed harder into the accelerator as the car's rear end drifted through each bank. As the hot rod entered a straightaway, he punched the pedal just so he could get the flathead to scream.

"Time's ticking." Dugan pulled out his father's silver pocket watch to check the time.

"Yes, I have other clients, Mr. Kolyok," the lawyer said.

With a sigh, Billy went to the table and set the binoculars down. "Where do I sign?"

The lawyer pointed with a pen to a solid line that required Billy's signature. "Here."

Billy took the pen and scribbled his name.

"You think a lot of Kash," Dugan said. He seemed especially cocky on this particular day, having inherited his father's entire fortune.

"I do."

The lawyer flipped several pages before landing on a space requiring another autograph.

"And you believe in him?" Dugan asked with a crooked grin.

"Whole-heartedly. He'll make a great driver."

"I don't want great. I want the best!" Dugan pointed. "I need him to win at Daytona this year."

"He'll be ready," Billy responded as he jotted down his name a second time.

"You sure about that?"

"Did you purchase the car, like I asked?"

"It's in the garage."

"Then it's a guarantee," Billy said. "Once Thomas sees it, he won't be able to resist."

"I'll have you know I spent a fortune on that car. And now NASCAR doesn't want it in any of their races. It's too powerful, they say."

"Leave that for Smokie to take care of," Billy replied.

"And last but not least," the lawyer interjected as he got to the last page, "one more."

Billy finalized the legal agreement. "There," he said. He'd taken a liking to the pen and placed it in his shirt pocket. "It's official. You now own me."

"And your debt, I might add," Dugan said. "From here on in, no more gambling!"

The lawyer scooped up the paperwork and placed it inside his briefcase. He removed a second contract and handed it to Billy.

"What's this?"

"A little insurance," Dugan said.

Billy glanced it over. "Another contract?"

"For Kash. He must agree to it if he wants to race."

"What if he refuses?"

"Then terminate him," Dugan said nonchalantly.

"Gentlemen," the lawyer urged. "If you'll excuse me, I have another appointment I must attend." He stood up and began to button up his jacket. "Mr. Kolyok." He extended a hand to Dugan who refused to even acknowledge him. "Oh well. Good day," he said and exited.

Billy folded Kash's contract in half and placed it inside his jacket. "I'm sorry about your father."

Dugan had an uncaring look in his eye.

The response irritated Billy, who contemplated the consequences of delivering a stiff backhand to his ungrateful new boss. "He was a good man. I only wish I could say the same for you."

Dugan grunted. "I'm not here to make friends. I'm here to make money."

Billy's anger intensified. "I made Chief a lot of money over the years."

Rising to his feet, Dugan rubbed his cheek with his forefinger, aggravated by the conversation. "Yes, my father said you could always draw a crowd. For your sake, I hope you still can."

The threat tempered Billy. He returned to the window and gazed out at the track.

"And one other thing," Dugan said, adjusting his tie.

Glancing over his shoulder, Billy made eye contact.

"Since I'm now in charge, you can address me as Chief. It has a nice ring to it."

"Your father received that title a long time ago because he was in charge of the pit crew. If you want me to call you that, you'll first have to earn it."

"Huh," Dugan scoffed. He turned and left.

"Bastard," Billy muttered under his breath. He banged his fist against the glass and looked out the window, spotting Kash and Nikki exiting the figure eight.

Chapter 18

Living up to his reputation as having a lead foot, Kash roared into the garage. He applied the emergency brake hard, locking up the rear wheels, making skid marks on the floor. Nikki braced herself against the dashboard. It was these antics that often drew Smokie's attention in the wrong kind of way.

As the Deuce stopped abruptly, Kash eyeballed Smokie's legs protruding from under a battered stock car. He grinned while revving the engine to get Smokie riled, but no response came. As he killed the engine, noise from a socket wrench cut through the mist of exhaust fumes. Kash hopped over the driver's door and headed to the passenger side, extending a hand to Nikki.

"See you later tonight, Thomas." She gave him a long kiss on the lips before exiting.

"Pick you up at seven." Kash turned to Smokie, who was likely eavesdropping. "Woo-wee, I think I set a new record." He slapped his hands together, feeling on top of the world.

"I told you before, fast cars and pretty women will lead to a shorter life," Smokie said.

"I wouldn't want it any other way." Kash peeked around the shop. It was crewless and disorganized, as if the men had left in a hurry. He leaned over the hood and peered down through the engine bay where he could see Smokie. "Where is everybody?"

"Gone home."

"So, what do you think of that old flathead? Purrs like a kitten, doesn't it?"

"If you keep driving her like there's no tomorrow, it'll soon sound like a dying cat." Smokie made more adjustments with the wrench.

"It's a hot rod. You're supposed to drive em' hard. Besides, if it breaks, I'll fix it." Kash reached down and pulled Smokie out by his feet as the wheels from the floor creeper squeaked.

"Hey!" Smokie aimed a finger at Kash. "You're really asking for it this time."

Kash removed his sunglasses and hung them from the neck of his T-shirt. "Gee, why are you all bent outta shape?"

"Have you forgotten we buried Chief this morning."

"I know," Kash replied, solemnly.

"Well, where the hell were you?"

"I was with Nikki."

Smokie sat up. "You know if Billy sees you speeding around in that tin can with his daughter, he'll spin your head like a nut on a threaded rod. She's the only thing he loves more in this world than racing."

"Well, that makes two of us."

"Oh, is that so. You're tellin' me you're in love with that girl?"

"As a matter of fact, I am. I've already asked her to marry me."

"Oh, brother. Did she laugh in your face?" He laid back down to resume his work.

Kash set his foot on the creeper to keep Smokie from moving. "She said yes."

"Really." Smokie propped himself up, using his elbows for support. "I didn't know she was that desperate."

"C'mon, Smokie. Quit busting my chops. I want you to be happy for me."

"Who says I'm not, kid?"

"And, I want *you* to be my best man."

"Best man, eh? You got the ole man's blessing?"

"Not yet. Still trying to muster up enough courage." He scratched the side of his head.

"That's you. As always, putting the cart before the horse."

"I suppose."

"Think she'll really be content hitching up with a grease monkey?"

Kash shook his head. "I got my sights set on bigger and better things."

"Like what?"

"Like winning races from behind the wheel."

"That so? Do you have a car you can enter? And I don't mean that thing." Smokie gestured at the roadster.

"Not at the moment, no."

"What about a signed contract?"

"Don't have that either." Kash was getting discouraged.

"Well, guess that settles it," Smokie said, nonchalantly. "You're just a grease monkey."

"Well, I am. I mean at least for now. But I'm not losing sight of my dream. And nobody's going to stop me."

"Who said anything about stopping you?"

"Besides, with Billy as my soon-to-be father-in-law, who knows what the future holds."

"Take it from me. The future will be here before you know it." Smokie tossed the tool aside and rubbed his arthritic hands. "I can't blame you for setting your sights higher. There comes a time in every man's life when turning a wrench loses its appeal. Now help me up."

Kash heaved him onto his feet. The demands of being a top mechanic in the racing circuit were taking their toll on Smokie, who showed signs of wear. He had deep lines on his face and dark circles under his eyes.

"You look a little tired. Everything okay?"

"I'm just an old warhorse who's getting long in the tooth." He wiped the grease from his hands with a shop rag pulled from his pocket. "Let's take a break and wet our whistles." Smokie limped over to a large work cabinet.

"What have you got in mind?" Kash followed alongside.

"A little firepower." Smokie reached inside a drawer and removed a bottle of whiskey and two small shot glasses. He sat them on a bench, filled them, and handed Kash his drink. "To love and happiness."

"To love and happiness," Kash repeated.

"And all the other headaches that go along with it."

Kash chugged down the shot. He choked on the harsh taste that took his breath away.

"Got a bite to it, doesn't it, kid?" Smokie laughed.

"What is this stuff?"

"It's high octane."

"Tastes like airplane fuel," Kash joked, wiping his lips with his hand.

Smokie poured himself a second. He offered Kash another, but he waved him off.

"I gotta ask you something," Kash said.

"I'm listening." Smokie rifled back another shot and leaned against the worktable to take the weight off his bad leg.

"I heard you tied the knot once."

"A long time ago."

"How come you're not married anymore?"

"Irreconcilable differences."

"Children?"

"Just one. A daughter. Haven't seen her since she was five. Be about your age now."

Smokie poured himself another drink. The mood of the conversation seemed to be on the downswing as Kash had hit a sore spot.

"What about racing?"

"What about it?"

"I heard you were pretty good."

Smokie's face went sour. He swallowed the alcohol down and banged the empty glass down on the tabletop. "I was."

"What happened?"

"This is what happened," he said, annoyed, eying his bum leg. "Biggest disappointment in my life. Cost me my career and marriage."

"I'm sorry. I shouldn't have asked."

"Forget about it." Smokie hobbled over to finish his work. "C'mon and give me a hand with this ole girl."

"Shouldn't the rest of the crew be helping? It's my day off."

"I told you. They've gone home."

"I don't get it."

"Let me spell it out for you, kid. They were all let go. That is except you and me, and Billy, of course.

"You're kidding, right?"

"Nope." Smokie lowered himself onto the creeper, groaning with every move. "Grab me a hammer."

Kash scooted over to a worktable and sorted through a pile of tools. He couldn't believe the rest of the team were fired.

"Your fiancé must have been blindsided by the proposal, or else she would have told you the news."

"She knew about this?" Kash located a hammer and returned.

"I suppose." Smokie got comfortable before using his good leg to propel himself under the car.

"But how can we race with half a pit crew?"

"The new owner has his own people."

"Huh." Kash spotted a heavy blue cotton tarp draped over a square-bodied automobile in the corner of the garage. "What's that?" He ventured over to take a closer look.

Smokie stopped his work. "I wouldn't touch that if I were you."

"I'm just looking."

"Right. Like a kid in a candy store."

Kash slid the cover back from the windshield. It was a brand new '65 Ford Galaxie stock car. The driver's side front fender was adorned with decals and 427 script. As he released the hood latch it made a popping sound.

"I said *hands off*," Smokie demanded.

Kash raised the hood and whistled aloud. The Ford big-block was unlike any motor Kash had ever seen. "Wow, would you look at that? Is this Billy's?"

"No."

"Is he racing at Daytona?"

"Not this year."

"Do you know what this is?" Kash asked with the utmost excitement.

"Yeah, it's a rocket ship on wheels."

"It'll be the baddest thing ever to hit NASCAR."

"If I get it ready in time. Now close the hood and pull the cover over before you get caught."

Kash glanced around the garage and saw a desk with a set of blueprints lying in full view. He wandered over, pulled a stool underneath his rear, and studied the drawings.

"I hope you're not looking at those diagrams."

"Nope," Kash said while holding back a chortle. "So, when do I get to go for a ride?"

"You don't."

"Why not?"

"'Cause, she's very expensive."

"I wish it were mine." Kash walked back to Smokie and stuck his head under the frame of the car. A trouble light shined from underneath. Smokie was staring at a bad tie rod, rubbing his chin.

"What are you doing under there, daydreaming?"

"Thinking."

"About what?"

"The consequences of setting this thing on fire instead of fixing it."

Kash chuckled as Billy approached from out of nowhere.

"Good day, gentlemen," Billy said.

Kash stood to face him. Smokie scampered out from under the chassis.

"Good afternoon," Kash replied, realizing Billy could have been eavesdropping on the conversation the whole time. He was now much taller than Billy, and lanky.

"How are things?"

"The usual calamities," Smokie said, pulling himself to his feet. "But I'll have her fixed in no time."

"Good." Billy turned his attention to Kash. "And how about Thomas?"

"Things are well, sir."

"I feel it was only yesterday you were hired to push a broom. Now look at you, a licensed mechanic." He looked at the souped-up Deuce with some concern. "And an avid race car driver too."

Kash feared a verbal reprimand.

"Soon I'll be competing against you."

"You know I wouldn't stand a chance," Kash replied, although he relished the idea of one day competing against his beloved mentor.

Billy noticed the '65 Galaxie, half exposed. "I see you've been nosing around."

"Who me? No, I mean not really." Kash glanced at Smokie, anticipating Billy would lose his cool at any second.

"Is that so?" Billy pulled the cover completely off the car and let it fall to the floor. He pointed to the driver's door where the name, Thomas Kash Jr., was written in yellow script. "What do you think?"

This must be some sort of practical joke, Kash thought. He rubbed his hand over the letters to see if they would wipe off. They didn't.

"It's for real," Billy said with assurance.

Smokie reached for a cigarette tucked inside his pocket. "I bet you didn't see that coming, eh kid?"

"I can't say I did." Kash stared on in disbelief.

"She's a beautiful machine, no?" Billy beamed with delight.

"Yeah, and I bet fast, too."

"So fast, it'll scare the pants right off you." Smokie reached into his coveralls for a lighter.

"Soon she'll be ready for Daytona. Isn't that right?" Billy asked.

"No doubt about it." Smokie stared at his bent cig.

"But will *you* be ready, Thomas?" Billy poked him hard in the chest.

"Yeah, sure, absolutely." Massaging away the pain, Kash was excited and nervous at the same time. He would have to keep this news an absolute secret from his mother.

Billy's enthusiasm grew as he shifted his attention to under the hood. "Tell him about the Cammer."

Smokie cupped his hands to light his smoke, then took a few puffs. "Well it's pretty much a standard 427 block with an enhanced oil system." He pointed out the particulars with his cigarette. "It's got a seven-and-a-half-quart oil pan, forged crank, and forged steel connecting rods, plus forged aluminum hemispherical domed pistons."

It was more information than Kash could process.

"Have you ever seen anything like it before, Thomas?" Billy asked.

"No, sir. Not even remotely." Kash rested against the front end, mesmerized by the mammoth V8.

"What about the top half?" Billy asked Smokie.

"That's where it gets even crazier. It's got free-flowing, cast iron cylinder heads, each with their own camshaft and lightweight intake valves for revs over seven grand. Keeping it all in sync are two timing chains, one of which is almost as tall as you. It's got a dual point distributor and a transistorized ignition amplifier to provide the exact fuel and air mixture for the twin four-barrel Holly carbs." Smokie took a drag. "It's got 12.0-to-1 compression, and over 600 horsepower. He stretched an arm inside the cabin and fired it up.

The sound was nothing like Kash had ever heard before. He felt exhilarated as Billy played with the throttle. The loudness nearly shook the tools off the bench as the exhaust pumped out a lumpy, chest-pounding rumble.

Surrounded by exhaust fumes, Smokie cut the engine.

Billy slapped Kash on the shoulder, nearly knocking him off his feet. "Tell me, Thomas. What do you think?"

"I think it'll eat Dodge for breakfast."

"Keep in mind, I have to de-tune it, somewhat," Smokie said, cringing.

"What?" Kash's mouth dropped open. He wanted all of it, just the way it was presented with all that unbelievable power.

"Otherwise, NASCAR won't allow it on the track."

"Why?"

"'Cause it's unbeatable," Billy replied as he placed a consoling arm around his young, impressionable new trainee. "So, we have to play by the rules."

"Don't worry, kid. She'll still be the fastest car on the track." Smokie dropped his cigarette and crushed it with the heel of his shoe.

"There's just one thing," Billy added.

"What's that?"

"You'll need a contract." He reached inside his jacket, pulled out the paperwork, and handed it to Kash who spread it on the front fender of the Galaxie and started to read it over.

"I even have a pen so you can sign it."

Kash sensed an urgency in his voice. Billy stood over his shoulder waiting impatiently.

"Can I at least read it first?" Kash asked.

"What's to read? Either you sign it, or else I have to terminate your employment."

"Are you kidding me?" The threat was like a death blow.

Billy shook his head. "Look, Thomas, the new owner spent a lot of time and money getting this car just for you to race."

"I understand that Billy, but it's all a bit overwhelming." He looked at Smokie, hoping for some words of advice. Smokie stood there, quiet, leaning against the driver's side door, eyes focused on the floor.

"It's a once-in-a-lifetime opportunity is what it is," Billy added.

"I realize that."

"It's your dream, isn't it? A chance to race professionally?"

"Yeah, no question about it," Kash said, nodding.

"Then what's the holdup?"

"I just want some time to look it over. Maybe consult my parents, or even a lawyer."

"This is the big leagues, Thomas. There's no time for negotiations. The new owner is expecting you to come through. He demands it."

It was happening all too fast and it gave Kash a headache. His options were limited and time was running out, but then he remembered his father's words about making the jump with both feet when the time was right.

"Well, what's it going to be?"

Kash reached for the pen in Billy's hand. He flipped a few pages of the contract and found the line that required his signature, then scribbled his full legal name and returned the document and pen to Billy.

"Now it's official. Congratulations." Billy ruffled Kash's thick, dark hair before taking the document, then walked to the drafting table and rolled up the blueprints before returning. "Here, take these."

"What are those?" Kash asked, playing dumb.

"The drawings you were looking at earlier. Memorize them. I want you to know every square inch of that car as if it was your own body." He stepped closer to him, and pointed a finger. "You be ready to race, you hear me?"

"I'll be ready."

Billy turned and proceeded to leave. He stopped just shy of the doorway, keeping his back to Kash. "And one more thing."

"Yes?"

"Racing has no passengers. You understand?"

"I do."

"Good. Then you have my blessing to marry my daughter." A second later, Billy disappeared out of sight.

Left standing in a state of euphoria, Kash pondered the welcome news as Smokie closed the hood on the Galaxie.

"Well, it looks like the future just showed up. First, a racing contract and now the old man's blessing. Two major milestones in one day."

Smokie grabbed the blue tarp and flung it over the car. He checked to make sure it was flat and even.

"Yeah." Kash wondered if signing the contract on the spot was the right thing to do. He turned to face Smokie. "You knew about this?"

"Sorry, kid, I was sworn to secrecy. Billy said I'd be fired if I let the cat outta the bag. C'mon. I could use another drink." Getting to the bench, Smokie poured himself a whiskey. "Want one?"

"No, you go ahead."

"Suit yourself." Smokie drank it straight up.

Knowing he had just been through a whirlwind, it finally dawned on Kash that he had failed to ask for one important piece of information. "Smokie, who's the new owner?" An ounce of fear resonated in his voice.

Smokie emptied the bottle as he poured himself the last pick-me-up.

"I asked you, who's the new owner?" Kash reached out and touched his best man's arm.

Smokie recoiled, "Dugan. Who else?"

Chapter 19

Donnie sat in a black leather chair across from Kash's desk. He was fidgety and crossed his legs back and forth while rubbing his hands.

"Yes, uh-huh, I understand. Alright, thanks for calling Doc." Kash sighed, tossed his cell on the desk, and rubbed his face.

"Well, how is he?" Donnie asked, nervously.

"He's stable."

"We should go see him." Donnie stood.

"Just sit tight. The doc says it was a severe anxiety attack. They're going to keep him overnight for observation. Right now, he just needs rest and no visitors."

"Alright." Donnie sat back down and reclined into the seat.

"Now, if we can talk shop for a moment."

"Oh, that reminds me." He pulled himself closer to the desk. "I received a message from a museum. They want to know if we'd be interested in selling off automotive artwork."

"Right now, I'd sell anything I could to pay off Dugan."

"I thought you might say that. I'll be sure to get in touch with them."

"Speaking of Dugan, he's on his way here, so don't get too comfy."

Donnie shot up. "I think I'll leave."

"Not so fast. I need your assistance." Kash strolled over to the antique safe, spun the tumbler back and forth a few times, then flipped the handle and pulled open the door.

Inside sat a quarter-million dollars stacked in even piles.

Kash withdrew the money and loaded it on his desk while Donnie checked the count.

"There's no money left," Donnie said as he glanced at the empty safe.

"I don't know what's worse. Seeing your business teetering on the brink of financial ruin, or selling the last of your possessions to try and stay afloat." Kash shook his head and sat down behind his desk.

"I guess this next sale could be it." Donnie's optimism dampened. "Should I inform the crew?"

"No. I'll break the news to them. Speaking of our next sale, do we have a feature car?"

"Not yet, but get this…"

"I'm all ears." Kash stroked his forehead with his fingertips.

"I got a call from a private collector who owns one of the original *Bullitt* movie cars."

"Okay, so…"

"So, he says he's thinking of selling it at auction. I've asked for a copy of the documentation, serial numbers, photographs, the usual kind of stuff."

"And?"

"It's legit."

Kash slapped his hands together. "Now that's our feature!"

"But, there's a problem."

"There always is," Kash said, momentarily deflated.

"I don't have him signed, but neither does anyone else for that matter."

"He wants a reserve on the car," Kash replied, speculating.

"A very high one. Ten million."

"Ten million!" Kash exclaimed. "Sounds like he isn't too eager to sell."

"That's why no auction house will take him seriously."

"I don't know anyone willing to pay that much, even if it is one of the *Bullitt* cars. Heck, the Batmobile sold for, what, four million?"

"Hammer price was four-point-two," Donnie replied.

Kash rested his elbows on the desk and ran the numbers in his head, thinking of the financial benefits of such a sale.

"The owner claims he's had offers as high as three-and-a-half million from a private collector," Donnie added.

"See if he'll reserve the car at four million."

"Not a chance. But even by some miracle if he went for it, do you think someone will pay that much?"

"Um, hard to say."

"And if it doesn't sell then we've wasted our time." Donnie folded his arms and exhaled heavily.

"Whether it sells or not, it'll be a major draw with buyers coming from across the globe. That alone could leverage into a few other sales."

"Already planning your next disaster, I see." Dugan strolled into the office wearing his long, dark Italian trench coat and a gentleman's hat. A cane, hinged from his elbow, swung back and forth in unison with his stride. The Mishka brothers accompanied him from behind—Abe held a thick document bound by a plastic spine and his brother Jonah, carried an empty duffle bag.

"Gentlemen, and I use the term loosely." Dugan sneered at Donnie who swallowed thickly.

"To what do we owe the honor?" Kash asked.

"Everything." Dugan rested his hat on the desk and waved to Jonah to hustle over and gather up the money.

"Aren't you going to count it?"

"I'm sure it's all there," Dugan replied slyly.

"I should let you two chat," Donnie said, poised to leave.

"Not so fast." Dugan pointed his cane against Donnie's chest. "I want you both to hear what I have to say." He eased into a chair next to Donnie, looking exhausted. "Aww. This is much better."

"You look like you've got one foot in the grave," Kash said.

"Never mind me." Dugan wiped the sweat from his pale face with a neatly folded cloth drawn from a pocket. "Let's get down to business."

"Is there a problem?"

"An epic one." Dugan leaned forward, grabbed the newspaper off the desk, and aimed a finger at the headline, "Kash and Kars Break More than Records!"

"After reading this morning's news, I have grave concerns about this company's future, and much more importantly, my money." Dugan tossed the paper to Kash.

"As far as I'm concerned, it's still business as usual."

"By the looks of that uninhabited safe, I'd say it's game over," he replied as Jonah finished up and joined his brother next to the doorway.

"You're forgetting we have another sale just around the corner."

Dugan smirked. "You still think you can pull a rabbit out of an empty hat. Hah!"

"If I can't, you'll take over."

"If there's anything left to take."

"Look Dugan, you'll get paid! Now, if there's nothing else, we have work to do."

"I don't brush off so easily." Dugan's eyes dug in hard. "The final payment is a cool million!" He glared at Donnie. "Can you pay it in full and on time?"

Donnie bit his lip and glanced at Kash. "Uh, well, I suppose we'll find out."

"Your former cellmate doesn't seem so confident," Dugan said, gloating. He used the cane to push himself back onto his feet. "But there is an easy way out." He gestured to Abe to deliver the legal papers.

Kash rolled his eyes. "How much more are you offering this time?"

Dugan grinned. "I'm offering less."

"Less."

"That's right. One-point-five million."

"A fifty percent drop!" Kash scoffed. "Now you're really hitting below the belt."

"It's a depreciating asset, facing an embarrassment of potential lawsuits by every ambulance-chasing lawyer in the state."

"Then I guess I should be thankful you showed up," Kash said sarcastically.

"Damn right. Quite frankly, I don't know anybody else that would buy you out at a time like this." He wandered over to the many accolades on display and paused to reflect. "It's not like the good ole days. Now, the world's full of odious vermin." Dugan began to cough. He pointed to the wet bar. "Bourbon, on the rocks," he said with difficulty breathing.

Kash nodded at Donnie.

"Okay, I'll get it."

The Mishka brothers watched closely as Donnie poured a tall glass of spirit and added a few cubes.

"Here's your poison," Donnie said smartly as Abe stepped forward to hand it off to Dugan.

With a harsh swallow, Dugan squinted in discomfort. "We've had an interesting working relationship all these years, haven't we?"

"Interesting. I suppose that's one word you could use to describe it. Financially, you fared much better than I."

"That's because I know how to play the game. And I always play to win. There was a time you did the same." He tapped the pane with his finger while staring at a color photo of Kash driving the '65 Ford Galaxie across the finish line. "I remember your first victory. It was one of many to come."

"And I remember sharing my earnings with you even back then."

"That's because you needed me," Dugan snickered. "Just like you do now." He examined the collage. "You competed against all the legends of motorsport and later became one yourself." He turned to face Kash. "Hell, you even gave Hollywood legend Paul Newman a run for his money."

"Paul had many talents. Racing was just one of them."

"Then you went from champion to car thief. Ever stop to think what happened in-between?"

"I know what happened. I was dealt a lousy hand and played it poorly."

"Things haven't gotten much better. Just look at you now. A glorified used car salesman at a run-of-the-mill auction company, selling the very same automobiles you once stole."

"I've been around cars my whole life. What else would I do?"

Dugan hobbled over to the office window overlooking the restoration shop, while taking small sips from his glass. "I'll have you know my associates thought I was crazy lending you a pile of money to start this venture. They placed bets on your imminent failure. Said you wouldn't last a year and I would lose my entire investment."

"How much did you bet against them?"

"A lot," Dugan said with pleasure. "I like playing the odds, especially when I can anticipate the outcome. The only flaw in your business plan is that you hired jailbirds to do the work of professionals." He pointed through the window. "Otherwise, I'm sure you wouldn't be in this predicament."

Donnie spoke up. "They're good people."

Dugan looked over his shoulder. "What was that?" He took a few steps toward Donnie and stared down at him.

"I'm just saying they're not to blame."

"Oh, that's grand coming from you. The great spin doctor, Donnie Kars. You're the worst of the bunch." He gripped Donnie's jaw hard, squashing it. "And the first I will personally dispose of."

Donnie broke free by twisting Dugan's wrist. "I wouldn't work for you anyway." He rubbed his sore chin.

"Good. That makes one less deadbeat I have to deal with." Dugan shook off the ache in his hand and nodded to Jonah, who strolled over and stood behind Donnie. He placed his huge hands over Donnie's shoulders, pushed him firmly into his seat, and squeezed hard.

Donnie struggled to break free. "What are you doing?" He let out a whimper as his eyes welled up and his body began to crumple.

It was unbearable to watch. It looked like Donnie was in a crusher at a wrecking yard. "Call him off, Dugan." Kash pounded his fist on the desk. "Damn it, you've made your point. Let him go!"

With a subtle nod from Dugan, Jonah backed off.

Donnie collapsed, exhausted.

"Now take what you came for and get out."

Dugan shuffled to the desk, set his drink down, and eyed Kash. "Swallow that foolish pride and pull your head out of your backside. You're finished!" He lifted his hat onto his head, then ambled towards Donnie. "And as for you…next time keep your big mouth shut."

The Mishka brothers stepped aside to let Dugan pass and they all exited out the door.

"You okay?" Kash asked his business partner.

"I feel like I've been put through a ringer." He managed to stretch his shoulders. "Is that how Dugan keeps his bodyguards in shape?"

"That's what they're paid to do." Kash lifted the legal document and briefly flipped the pages.

"What are you gonna do?" He asked while continuing to massage his neck.

"Honestly, I'd like to know what you and the crew want. Whether to throw in the towel, or fight to the bitter end."

"I want what everybody else here wants." His eyes grew big. "To watch Dugan lose."

Picking up Dugan's papers and glancing at Donnie, Kash tossed them into the garbage.

Chapter 20

It was a cool, brisk morning at the Brickyard on May 31, 1965. Cars lined the track at the Indianapolis Motor Speedway for the 49th International 500 Mile Sweepstakes. The stands were crammed with fans, from the diehard to the shameless that came for the carnage. Some shouted obscenities, others sang tunes from the top of their lungs, but most sat quietly sipping away at a soft drink or scoffing down junk food while waiting patiently for the race to begin.

Sitting in the nosebleed section, with binoculars in hand, Kash nuzzled alongside his wife, Nikki, who was eight months pregnant. She didn't like watching from the pits due to the noise, and was equally dissatisfied with her location in the public viewing area. Kash did his best to keep her content, however, he was eager to meet up with Billy, who was competing that day.

The fans rose to their feet and cheered as the race got started. Billy held the pole position as the cars roared past at breakneck speeds, tossing up fragments of debris from their rear tires.

Before long, the temperature had climbed. It was going to be a hot one. Kash peeled off his jacket and kicked back. To make the day more entertaining, Nikki challenged her husband to a game of prediction. They both took turns guessing which car might blow an engine or lose control. It was a break from an otherwise repetitive day for Kash, who hated to be parked on the bench.

By early afternoon, a steady breeze had settled in and Billy started to fall behind. Kash suspected car trouble and, feeling restless, he left Nikki's side to visit the pits. There, he noticed Smokie standing alone, dressed in white coveralls with red vertical stripes that ran up the side. He had one foot planted on a barrier as he puffed away on a cigarette. A small flask poked out of his other hand.

Kash grabbed a pair of earmuffs resting on a nearby cart as he strolled by, gazing at the crew that looked mostly unfamiliar to him. It was no secret that Dugan struggled to keep any employees onboard longer than a few months.

"Hey there!" Kash shouted, drawing attention.

Smokie's face reddened with embarrassment. He slipped his drink into a pocket and wiped his mouth. "How are you, kid?"

"Just fine, but it looks like Billy's having some difficulty."

"Yeah. I'm not sure what the problem is, but speak of the devil, here he comes now." Smokie pointed to Billy's mid-engine Lotus 38 as it headed for a pit stop, kicking up enough dust that the team had to shield their eyes. When the red and white monocoque-bodied race car came to an abrupt halt, Billy exploded. "The accelerator keeps sticking on this damn thing!"

Additional pit crew members moved in to change the rear tires as Smokie scurried off for a can of oil. Kash stepped forward to give a warm hello, but Billy cut him short.

"I need to speak to you." He pointed at him. "It's important."

"After you win," Kash responded with a thumbs up.

He shook his head. "You need to watch out!"

"For who?" He wasn't sure who Billy was referring to, and Smokie abruptly pushed Kash aside to confront Billy. It was hard to overhear the conversation with all the surrounding noise, but it was apparent to Kash that the once dream team was now arguing with fingers pointing at each other.

"Tell that bastard I won't race for him anymore!" Billy shook his fists.

"You can't throw in the towel. There's too much at stake!" Smokie moved away to examine the throttle lever on the carbs.

Kash watched closely as Smokie manually operate the butterfly valves on the carburetors by hand as extreme heat blasted off the manifolds.

"Can you fix it or not?" Billy shouted over his shoulder as the throttle whined down. He didn't get an answer. Now, more angered, he banged his knuckles off the side of the car as the crew finished putting on a new set of rubber. "Let's go! Let's go!"

"Hold your horses!" Smokie lubed the moving parts with spray as a breeze carried some onto the hot engine, which sent puffs of smoke up into the air. He moved the mechanical levers back and forth one last time as the engine ran in tune. Kash realized it was time to get out of the

162

way and he stepped back just in time before Smokie whacked the side of the car with a rag to signal Billy to leave.

In a fit of rage, Billy stomped on the gas and laid a long patch of rubber as he beelined for the track.

Alarmed, Kash confronted Smokie. "Are you crazy? That spray is going to dry up in no time. Then what's Billy going to do?"

Smokie shrugged it off. "You worry too much, kid. Billy won't forfeit the race on account of a sticky throttle."

Kash shook his head. It was a risk not worth taking. It was just too dangerous to maintain full speed on the straightaways at over 150 mph!

"And here comes Billy the Kid in car number sixty-nine," the announcer exclaimed over the loudspeakers.

Viewing the race through his binoculars, Kash spotted the Lotus slowly gaining ground on a pack of cars ahead. With just a few more laps to go, Billy was gunning towards the front of the line. He squeezed his way in between cars, at times touching tires with his adversaries. Entering the southeast corner, a strong gust forced one of the slower cars up front to swerve, nearly causing a collision. A skillful master at his profession, Billy made the maneuver look easy. There were now just two cars ahead of him. The crowd began to stand up and go wild, but it was still anybody's race.

Just short of the finish line, Billy rocketed into the final turn as Kash kept a watchful eye. A second later, his car began to slide sideways where screeching tires created a smokescreen for drivers following behind.

"And Billy the Kid's in trouble!" the announcer cried out.

The Lotus then flipped upside down and skidded down the track. Fuel poured out on the hot engine and flames erupted.

"Number sixty-nine has just suffered a serious wipeout and has caught fire!"

A small cluster of cars skirted around the accident, but one driver panicked and veered into another, causing a violent chain reaction. One by one, they skidded out of control, banging into the guardrail and smashing into each other like they were in a high-speed demolition derby.

"Oh my gosh! There's now a colossal pileup happening," the announcer added.

Screams from the crowd rang out as crushed sheet metal and parts littered the track. The cars fell like wounded soldiers spread across an open battlefield.

"And the yellow flag has been dropped with over thirty wrecked cars scattered across the field! What a frightening scene this is, ladies and gentlemen!"

"Snap out of it, kid!" Smokie demanded as he jolted Kash, who couldn't believe what he had just witnessed. The two jumped into a nearby tow truck and sped a half a mile down the track to where Billy's car sat upside down, ablaze.

Steering around the wreckage, Kash saw no movement from inside the car. He could barely breathe and his heart thumped so loud it pulsated in his ears. Smokie exited the tow truck with a fire extinguisher in hand as black smoke billowed out from the Lotus. He dampened the flames as Kash rushed to Billy's aid.

Kneeling on the hot asphalt, Kash peered into the cockpit. Billy's body was pinned with his head flopped to one side. Blood dripped from his nose. "Billy, can you hear me?" Kash could see Billy's eyes were open, but there was no response. He stuck his arm through a small gap and grabbed Billy, then shook him. He didn't stir.

"Billy!" Kash cried out as fire trucks and an ambulance arrived on scene to assist, but it was too late. The once charismatic and brilliant race car driver, Billy the Kid, was dead.

Chapter 21

Kash signaled as he steered the dark, ivory-green '70 Boss 429 into a derelict speedway. He drove across an empty lot and through an open section of fence that gave way to an oval track absent of any buildings.

The engine thumped out a lumpy idle as the car came to a stop in the center of the road. Tightening his black leather driving gloves, he took a good look at his surroundings.

Most of the buildings were long gone. The grandstands had become overgrown by trees. Tall weeds shot up through the cracks in the asphalt and deep ruts scarred the surface of the track. It was far from ideal for a road test, but it would have to do.

The Boss sounded better than ever with its tuneful idle. Kash gave it a few shots of gas, then dumped the clutch and hammered the accelerator, spinning both rear tires in smoke and a screeching blast that could have been heard for miles.

As he shifted from one gear to the next, the speedo quickly climbed over 120 mph. Circling the track, Kash sliced through the wildflowers that lay in his path. Once there were none left, he slowed the muscle car down, slid into a half-circle, and headed back in the opposite direction, using every last bit of horsepower.

After a ten-minute thrill ride, he decided to call it quits. His cell rang and Donnie's name flashed on the display. He didn't answer as it would disrupt his fun away from the office.

About twenty minutes later, as the sun was about to set, Kash finished his test drive by barreling down the driveway towards the rear of the restoration shop. The Boss hugged every turn before coming to a stop outside a bay door.

All of the crew had already left for the day except Donnie, who was waiting outside to greet Kash.

"Out joyriding like some over-the-hill adrenaline junky." Donnie shook his head.

"Just making sure everything's tip-top," Kash replied.

"Sure you were," he snickered. "So, how's it handle?"

"Nose-heavy, but hauls ass." He held up the keys on the end of his finger. "You wanna take her for a spin?"

"Would love to, but I don't think the client would appreciate it."

The remark sounded scolding, Kash thought, but his business partner had a point.

"I tried calling to let you know your latest acquisition is here," Donnie said.

"Where is it?"

"On the hoist."

He stepped around Donnie, anxious to see the new arrival.

"Still can't figure out why you spent the last of your savings on that heap."

"And I couldn't begin to explain to you the importance of it all."

"I suppose you're right," Donnie replied. "You mind closing up?"

"No problem. Go home and get some rest. See you tomorrow."

As the two parted, Kash immediately headed inside.

And there it sat. A tormented-looking '65 Lotus 38 on four deflated Firestone tires.

Kash stared at it in utter disbelief. It was the car that claimed Billy's life. Sadly, it bared little resemblance to its once glorious condition. He walked down one side of the car and gently touched it, as if reaching out to his old friend. Closing his eyes for a moment, the images of that dreadful day repeated themselves.

Reawakened by the painful thoughts, Kash raised the lift high enough to stand underneath the vintage racer. He snatched a trouble-light lying on the floor and hung it from the front end, walked under the chassis, and began examining every detail.

By early morning, sunlight had crept above the horizon and through the open bay door. Kash was checking over the engine when he heard footsteps.

"For the love of God." Dugan thumped his cane against the floor.

"What brings you here?"

He walked past, fixated on the roadster. "It can't be."

"I'm afraid it is," Kash said, his voice heavy with emotion.

Dugan wiped his face with a handkerchief. He was already sweating. For a man of fearless conviction, he appeared shaken. "Where did you unearth this corpse?"

168

"Resting in a derelict stable." Kash gazed around. "Where's your entourage?"

"I came alone so we could talk in private."

"You mean by yourself?" He suspected the Mishka brothers might be close by and he glanced around, trying to spot them.

"Well, I did bring the Peacemaker." He pushed his long trench coat to one side and flashed a .45-caliber pistol. Its ivory handle shined from its holster.

"Of course," Kash replied, thinking he could be bound, gagged, and disposed of at any moment without a single eyewitness.

Dugan gazed at the series of parts strewn across the floor. "That's quite an autopsy."

"Just trying to find out what happened."

"Everybody knows what happened. Billy sped too fast into the turn and lost control. The car flipped and he died instantly." Dugan extended an arm and tapped the side of the car. "It's a damn shame."

"Billy didn't make a mistake."

Dugan raised an eyebrow. "Is that so?" He used his finger to flick off a piece of dried mud clinging to the side of the roadster.

"The throttle was stuck open." Kash cleaned his hands with a rag and tossed it aside.

"Not unheard of. I recall the same thing happened to another driver." He snapped his fingers repeatedly. "What was his name?"

"Roger McCluskey," Kash replied as he vividly remembered hearing about the mishap back in '65.

"Correct. Although he survived, his Lotus was completely destroyed. Yet you believe this one to be an act of sabotage."

"I have my suspicions."

"And why's that?" He poised his cane in front of him and leaned on it with one hand over the other.

"'Cause when you're on top, there's always someone trying to knock you down."

"I'll give you that one."

"And the fact the car disappeared without a trace right after the accident."

"I had it hauled away to be crushed," Dugan said.

"To hide the evidence."

Outraged, Dugan banged his fist off the nose of the car. "Because it took the life of one of the greatest race car drivers that ever lived! Its presence was nothing more than a painful reminder—as it is now." He then pointed at the roadster. "Yet through some miracle, here it lies."

"I like to think it's karma."

"If you believe in that kinda thing." He sat down on a stool across from Kash and rested a hand on his pistol. "You're just wasting valuable time."

Kash raised his voice. "I want to know the truth, for once and for all!"

"Knowing the truth can come with a hefty price."

"After all these years, I'd say you owe it to me."

"I owe you nothing." Dugan withdrew a pair of black leather gloves from his coat and slid them over each hand. He grasped his gun.

A sinking feeling washed over Kash, but he pretended not to let it show. "I was there, in the pits, that day when Billy wheeled in. He was enraged. Said he wouldn't race for you anymore."

"Billy was always a hothead. He was just letting off steam."

"He also told me to watch my back."

"That's good advice for anyone." Dugan opened the cylinder, made sure each chamber was loaded, and slapped it closed. He wiped down the handle before holstering the gun.

"The next thing I knew, Billy headed back onto the track."

"A decision that proved fatal."

"I don't think he had much choice in the matter."

"Nonsense. He could have chosen to withdraw from the race."

"I heard he owed money all over, and even left a few debts behind for you to cover," Kash prodded.

"More than a few," Dugan replied sharply. "At least one in every state he raced, and to people a lot less forgiving than me." He pushed himself onto his feet. He was shaky for a few steps as he began to circle the car.

"How much did he owe?"

"Enough that he could never pay it off in short order. That's why I took the liberty of handling his financial affairs."

"You owned him."

"You bet I did," he said arrogantly. "He raced exclusively for me. I also gave him protection from the guys that wanted to bust his skull when he couldn't pay up. I did the same for you when you were in prison, remember?"

"But he never stopped gambling, did he?"

"No." Dugan shook his head. "Nothing could stop Billy from doing what he wanted."

"And here was a way out. An accident in the making and a chance for you to collect on the insurance."

"Nothing could be further from the truth. Billy was still a guaranteed moneymaker. And you never hurt the golden goose, even when he becomes a royal pain in the ass, just like you, Kash."

"But you did have a successor in mind."

"In this business, you have to in order to stay alive. It only made sense to put you behind the wheel. After all, you were trained by the best."

"And I've been your golden goose ever since."

"Damn right. I made millions off you, and I'm not ashamed to say it."

"Quite frankly you still are."

"That's because I've always been great at picking winners."

"Soon you'll have to find yourself another."

"Huh," Dugan scoffed. "You and I are like two cogs in a machine." He entwined his fingers. "One can't work without the other, but together, they make perfect harmony."

"If you didn't arrange for Billy's death, then who did?" Kash asked point-blank.

"Who else?" He poked his head over the driver's side. The interior was still complete, but filled with dirt, dust, and an awful mustiness. Dugan waved a hand in front of his nose before glancing over to Kash. "It was Smokie."

"That's a helluva thing to say."

"Is it? How do you think he got that bum leg?"

"From an accident in '53 at the Detroit Motor Speedway."

"Billy was to blame for that. Did you know?"

"No," Kash replied, arms folded, as he leaned against the hoist. "Smokie didn't like to talk much about his past."

172

"He would have had a very promising career if Billy hadn't intentionally clipped the back end of his car that day." He sighed at the thought.

"How do you know all this?"

"When I was a kid, my father liked to tell tales, most of which were neither here nor there, except he liked to tell this particular one quite often."

"What happened?"

"Smokie lost control and skidded straight into the wall. Long story short, he was lucky to be alive, but his right hip and leg were broken in four places. Doctors said it would be a miracle if he ever walked again."

"So Smokie couldn't race anymore. He at least had a second career as a top-notch mechanic."

"That's not how he saw it," Dugan fired back. "Smokie wanted to be on the track to beat Billy at his own game."

"Yet the two partnered up because it was in their best interest."

"It was in my father's best interest! He saw great potential in pairing up a brilliant mechanic and a gifted driver as a recipe for winning races. But deep down, little did any of us know, Smokie had a score to settle."

"You want me to believe that Billy was bushwhacked by his own teammate. And not just any member of his crew, but his right-hand man."

"You wanted the truth and I'm giving it to you."

"Even if Smokie resented Billy for what happened, why would he wait more than a decade to seek revenge?"

"Revenge is a dish best served cold."

Kash pondered Dugan's explanation as he watched him move about the room.

"Smokie lived in pain every day while the cars he built took Billy to the number one position—the same man responsible for ending his own racing career." He wiped away the filth that hid the driver's initials painted on the body of the car. "Billy became famous," he pointed out. "Smokie, unknown. A few days after the accident, I had this terrible feeling come over me. The kind that creeps up on you, wakes you up at night, and ties your stomach in knots. For the life of me, I couldn't figure out what it was. Then, it dawned on me."

"What'd you do?"

"About a week after Billy died, I had Smokie meet me in my office after hours. He was jittery, couldn't even look me in the eye. It was a challenge just to make small talk with the man."

"You telling me he spilled his guts to ya."

"At first he denied any wrongdoing. Acted all innocent, even sobbed retelling the story of Billy's accident. He put on a good front for several hours and was a tough ole buzzard, but I was tired of hearing him sing the same old tune. I needed to turn up the heat if I was going to get anywhere."

"You beat him, didn't you?"

"Within an inch of his life, before he caved."

"Jesus," Kash murmured, knowing Dugan would have taken pleasure in delivering punishment.

"I did what was necessary, and in the end, I got a confession. But I gotta hand it to him though. His plan was almost flawless. Likely would have pulled it off too, had I not remembered that story about his own misfortune."

"You destroyed him."

"For Christ's sake, he earned it. He took Billy's life and almost turned my entire enterprise completely upside down. He could no longer be trusted and was a danger to everyone, including you!"

"Smokie never caused me any harm."

"I wasn't going to wait around to find out." He dabbed the small beads of perspiration from his forehead. "I told him to leave town, and if he ever showed his face, I'd finish him."

"You did. Six months later, he met his fate in a head-on collision with a cement truck."

"Now *that's* karma."

"More like an eye for an eye. The truck was stolen. No prints. No witnesses. And never any arrest."

"It's a 'whodunit' mystery," Dugan boasted.

"I think we both know whodunnit."

"Listen to me, Kash." He pointed with his cane. "There's no point in digging up ancient history. We're all that's left now. The rest are all dead and forgotten."

"I'm not about to forget about Billy, or Smokie."

"You best let it go for your own good, you hear me?" Dugan circled back and sat back down on the stool, arms crossed, steely-eyed. He leaned over, coughed, and spat on the floor.

Kash saw Donnie quietly enter through the double doors to the restoration shop. They made brief eye contact as Donnie caught a glimpse of Dugan and ducked back out of sight.

"First thing you need to do is scrap this car. It's a bad omen." He coughed again.

"Need something?"

"No, it'll pass." He hacked into a handkerchief. When he pulled it away from his mouth Kash saw that it was spotted with blood.

"Now that looks serious."

Dugan folded it up and put it away. "I have lung cancer."

"Foregoing treatment?"

Dugan nodded.

"How much time you got left?"

"Not enough."

"And you still want my business."

"What can I say? I'm an opportunist. In fact, I'll sweeten the pot. Fifty-fifty. Just you and me, for old time's sake. What do you say?"

"And Donnie?"

"Get rid of him."

"Do you propose a jammed accelerator or a cement truck?"

"I could care less how you do it. Just make it happen while I'm still kickin'," Dugan said slyly.

"I think it's time for you to leave." Kash pressed a button on the hoist and the race car began to lower to the ground.

"Have it your way." He pulled out the gun and pointed it at Kash. His arm wavered and his hand trembled, making it impossible to keep aim.

"What the hell are you doing?" Kash stopped the lift. "I thought you said you wouldn't hurt the golden goose, even when he's a pain in the ass?"

"Best step aside." Dugan pulled the hammer back and opened fire. The sound was deafening as the first shot grazed Kash's left shoulder before he dove behind a set of new Firestones. The second bullet pierced the front end and a third shattered the already-cracked windshield. A fourth shot hit the rim of the rear tire. For good measure, he fired two more rounds. One bullet ricocheted off the spaghetti-looking exhaust pipes and struck a nude pin-up calendar hanging on the wall. The other passed over the car, went straight out the open bay door, and took out a headlight on the Boss. He pulled the trigger again but the six-shooter was empty.

Ears ringing, Kash stepped in front of the roadster and discovered Donnie on all fours, nearly frozen with fear, peeking around a tool chest.

Dugan was busy reloading his gun.

"What the hell you do that for?" Kash asked.

"For climactic release," Dugan replied as smoke from the pistol wafted in the air.

Kash glanced at the tear in his clothing where the bullet sliced through, skinning his arm.

"I hope that wasn't your favorite shirt."

"Would it matter?"

"Not to me."

"I didn't think so." He evaluated the trajectory of all the rounds. "I'm relieved. Overall you're a terrible shot."

"Perhaps. But now that I have your full attention, we can discuss the solvency of our relationship." Dugan holstered his weapon. "Do you have my money?"

"I will, like always," Kash replied. "A few days after the auction."

"I'm interested to learn your strategy to raise that much capital in such a short time."

"It's a work-in-progress."

"Still putting the cart before the horse," Dugan sneered.

"It'll be a show-stopper."

"Like last time, I'm sure." He tapped Kash on the elbow to signal him to step aside. As Dugan made his way under the large bay door, he stopped and glanced over his shoulder. "And, just so there's no misunderstanding, you are no longer my golden goose. In my mind, you are quite simply emblematic of this once, truly magnificent race car, now long overdue for the scrap yard. Good day." He tipped the brim of his hat and exited.

Kash headed towards the double, swinging doors that led to his office. He held his wound tightly as Donnie popped up.

"Kash!"

"For crying out loud, Donnie. Don't sneak up on me like that!"

"I'm sorry." He spotted the blood seeping through Kash's top. "You've been hit!"

"It's only a scratch."

"Are you sure?"

"Yeah, I'll be fine."

Donnie looked at the roadster. A cloud of blue smoke hovered above it. "He's not playing around anymore, is he?"

"Don't think he ever was."

"What are we going to do?"

"The only thing we can do. Make sure we pay him in full. And pray he never returns."

Chapter 22

Kash wandered across the third floor of the hospital with a shopping bag in hand. From one room to the next, he poked his head inside in hopes of finding Rev. In one spot there was a young woman parked in front of a television, in another an elderly person asleep on a chair. There were patients everywhere, but no sign of Rev.

Rounding a corner, Kash nearly bumped into a man using a walker who was exiting a bathroom. "Sorry," he said before shuffling down the hall to where he saw Rev wrapped in a light blue hospital gown, sitting on the edge of a bed, legs draped over the side. "Ah, there you are." He stepped forward. "How you feeling?"

"Like a hundred dollars." Rev stared at the floor.

"You look restless." Kash took a long, hard look at him and for the first time saw a helpless-looking old man.

"I'm as fidgety as a mouse in a tin outhouse."

"How come?"

"Upset stomach." He rubbed his gurgling belly.

Kash reached into the bag and pulled out a framed photograph which he placed on the nightstand next to Rev.

"What's this?" He picked it up.

"It's a gift from the crew."

Rev stared at it. Each member had signed a get-well wish.

"Tell the gang thanks," he said, tearing up before setting the present aside.

"I will. Do you want me to get the nurse?"

"I already buzzed her, twice."

"Is there something I can do for you?"

Rev looked at Kash awkwardly. "You ever give an enema?"

"Nope."

"Good answer."

A sense of humor was a good sign. Kash tossed the bag onto the bed. "Well I brought you some fresh clothes."

"Coveralls," Rev said as he peeked inside the bag.

"It's not like I have keys to your apartment."

Rev placed the clothing over his lap. "It's redneck fat-wear."

"Isn't that your brand?" Kash joked.

Rev groaned as he lay back in bed.

"Maybe you need more rest."

He bent his knees to help keep him from sliding down the bed. "Don't leave. I wanna talk to you."

"Okay." Kash took a seat in a nearby chair. "What's on your mind?"

"Am I fired?" Rev asked as he made himself a bit more comfortable while staring up at the ceiling.

Kash thought about it for a second. "Nah, you're not fired."

"Why not?"

"You say that as if you're disappointed?"

"The Corvette was stolen because I left the keys in it."

"Maybe so."

"And I was way outta line with Jalopy."

Kash nodded in agreement. "And Soney, too."

"Tell them I didn't mean to bust their chops."

Kash hung his head for a second. "You can tell them yourself, when you're ready to come back to work."

"I'm ready now. Doc says I can leave anytime." Rev rolled onto one side, close to the edge of the mattress, and gently slid his legs over before sitting upright.

"You telling me that because you hate hospitals?"

"Kinda." He looked him straight in the eye. "Why do you care what happens to me anyway? I've had three wives in my life and not one of them ever gave a damn."

"'Cause the place wouldn't be the same without you," Kash said warmly.

"Balderdash."

"Alright. The guys need you." Kash pointed at the photo.

"You never made a good liar," Rev exhaled loudly as if trying to release the gas that remained trapped inside his belly.

"If you want the truth, I'm in a tough spot. In fact, I stand to lose it all."

"Dugan got you by the short and curlies?" He clenched his fist and winced as if to illustrate a torturous ball squeeze.

"I'm afraid so."

"That's what happens when you make deals with the devil."

"I can't disagree with you on that one."

"Give me a hand up."

Kash extended his arm to offer support. "Let me help you get dressed."

"I got it," Rev grumbled as he began to slip on his coveralls.

"Don't you want to remove that gown first?"

"Do you really want me to do that right here?"

"Not really."

"I didn't think so." Rev slipped on his workwear. He grabbed his gift and tossed it into the bag. "Let's go." He headed out the door as Kash trailed behind.

"Hey, what about your enema?"

"Let 'em shove it up someone else's backside," Rev replied. "C'mon, let's get the hell outta here."

Chapter 23

After returning from hospital, Kash sauntered into his office where the team was waiting.

Gazing thoughtfully out the window to the restoration bay was Soney. He toyed with the lid of an old Zippo lighter, repeatedly flipping it open and closed.

Jel sat in one of the fine leather chairs, adjacent to Miss Sabrina. He was glancing through an old issue of *Mechanics Illustrated.* Miss Sabrina was in her own little world too, preoccupied with texting on her cell phone.

Donnie stood against the bar, drink in hand. A bottle of Drambuie sat nearby. He looked half-cocked and rattled the cubes in his glass.

Leaning next to the trophy case stood Cosmo and Flywheel, arms crossed, not saying a word and staring down at the floor. Expressions were glum, like they were paying their respects at a funeral.

Rev staggered in and headed towards Donnie.

"Good to have you back, Rev," Donnie said with sincerity. "We'll need everyone on board this time."

"Wouldn't miss it for the world."

"You want a drink?"

"Just water for me, thanks."

Donnie quickly filled a small glass from behind the bar and handed it to Rev.

With the crew together, Kash cleared his throat to draw attention. Surprised faces peered up at him.

"Good afternoon. It looks like we have everyone here so we'll get started. First of all, I want to welcome back our friend and colleague." He motioned, and all heads turned to see Rev with a raised drink in hand.

"We missed you, Rev," Miss Sabrina said with a wink.

"I missed you too, darling."

"I'll get straight to the point." Kash sat on the lip of the desk. "This next sale will either make us or break us."

"I don't understand." Miss Sabrina brushed her bangs away from her face. "I thought we were doing okay."

"The attempted robbery of the Corvette put a monkey wrench in our purse strings," Donnie announced. Appearing bothered by the constant clicking of the lighter, he strolled over and snatched it from Soney, who remained deadpan. "We lost thousands of dollars in sales."

"Right now, the bigger problem is Dugan." Kash stroked his chin and exhaled.

"Who's Dugan?" Miss Sabrina asked.

"The fella that tried to make Swiss cheese outta that Lotus," Donnie pointed in the direction of the restoration shop.

184

"Why would someone shoot up an old race car? That's insane." She nibbled away at a hangnail.

"Word has it that you were hit by one of the stray bullets," Jel spoke up.

"Rest assured, it was nothing serious."

"Once again, who's Dugan?" Miss Sabrina pleaded.

"A silent business partner who helped finance this operation in the beginning. But I have no plans to continue our relationship once he is fully remunerated after our next sale."

"How much do you owe him?" Cosmo scratched his forehead. "If I may ask?"

"The final payment is a million dollars."

"Whoa!" the group cried out together.

"Now calm down," Kash ordered. "I did the math and we got a shot at pulling this off."

Flywheel perked up. "It sounds like we could all be looking for work."

"That's right," Cosmo chirped in. "Guess we should start brushing up our resumes. I hear prison time's always a big draw for employers."

The gang of ex-cons all grumbled in commiseration.

"Let's not get ahead of ourselves," Kash urged. "We need to focus on the *now*."

"How many cars must we sell?" Soney asked, shifting his gaze from the shop floor to Kash.

Kash massaged the back of his neck, knowing the next words out of his mouth would create tension. "Every darn one of them."

"And how many is that?" Flywheel asked.

"At least two hundred."

The crew moaned.

"Now hold on. Just hold on, everybody! Let's keep our heads in the game. Most of the entries will have no reserve."

Flywheel wiped his brow. "I'm not sure we can push through that many in just one day."

"We have to," Kash said. "Or else we stand to lose it all."

"That's a lot of cars to sell." Cosmo scratched the side of his head.

"How many consignments do we currently have?" Jel asked.

"One eighty-eight by this morning's count." Donnie sucked on an ice cube before spitting it back into the glass.

"So, we need another twelve cars to consign by this Friday," Jel said.

"At least, but with Donnie and I reaching out to every prospective client, we hope to exceed that number, just in case there are dropouts."

"What's the feature car?" came a female voice from the doorway. Heads turned to view Sandra Kash, dressed in high heels, a tight black mini-skirt, and matching top. A stylish handbag hung from her shoulder.

"C'mon in," Kash said in surprise as he stood up and waved his daughter over.

"Wow!" She had Donnie's full attention.

Sandra was stunning in contrast to her nearly all-male audience—like a Bentley rolling through a scrapyard. She approached Kash and gently planted a kiss on his cheek. "You didn't come home last night, dad. I was getting worried."

"I was here, putting in some long hours."

Sandra lifted the newspaper off the desk and glanced at the headline—"Kash and Kars Break More than Records!"

"I reported it stolen," she admitted regretfully.

186

"I'm sorry. I should have told you I planned on taking it to auction."

"Forget about it." She tossed her purse aside. "For now, let's talk business."

"I was hoping you'd say that. I could use some fresh ideas. I believe you know just about everyone, except Jel, our new mechanic, and Miss Sabrina, our co-op student."

"Finally, another female," Miss Sabrina said, relieved. "I was getting nauseous from all the testosterone."

"I know what you mean." Sandra giggled. "But trust me, it'll grow on you."

"I like her already," Miss Sabrina replied.

Sandra shifted her attention to Donnie. "So, what's our feature?"

"The *Bullitt* Mustang." As the words rolled off Donnie's tongue, a bolt of excitement recharged the team.

"The *Bullitt*!" Cosmo gasped.

Finally, a glimmer of hope, Kash thought. He was delighted to watch their frowns wash away.

"I signed him this morning."

"Great work." Kash rubbed his hands together.

Donnie raised his near-empty glass. "Here's to me." He took a gulp and polished off the remaining alcohol.

"Hold up," Sandra interrupted. "Is there a reserve?"

The room went quiet as faces tensed like they were all wrestling with constipation.

"Yeah, of course. It was the only way I could get the owner to sign."

"How much?" Sandra asked.

"It's alright," Kash assured her. "Donnie and I have already discussed the reserve."

"I wanna hear it from him."

Donnie looked over at Rev. "And I thought I asked the tough questions."

"You gonna tangle with the boss's daughter, you better be prepared."

"Well, how much?" Sandra pushed him hard.

"Four million, right Donnie?" Kash asked as he saw a look of unease in Donnie's eyes. He suspected something wasn't right.

"You're kidding me," Sandra replied. "That's way too high."

Donnie's cheeks flushed as he crunched on another piece of ice. "Actually five."

A groan rang out from the crew as their chances seemed to fade.

"Here, let me get you another drink," Rev said as chatter broke out. He reached for the bottle of Drambuie and poured Donnie a stiff one.

It was like a hit below the belt for Kash.

"I guess that's his 'not for sale' price," Sandra scoffed.

"I thought we discussed this," Kash said, disheartened.

"He wouldn't go any lower. It was the best I could do, and I got him signed."

"We're gonna need another feature," Kash said to Sandra as the discussions in the room grew louder.

Sandra whistled to silence the group. "Okay," she said, whipping her hair back. "What else we got?"

The gang stared back with blank expressions.

"What do you mean?" Donnie asked. "That *is* the feature car."

"And if the *Bullitt's* a dud, then what?"

The center of attention swung to Donnie. He cleared his throat and appeared to be stumped.

She threw her hands up into the air. "I can't believe this. He doesn't even have a backup."

Donnie held out his glass for another round as Rev topped him off.

Kash saw that look in his daughter's eyes. She was engaged, running full throttle and taking charge.

"C'mon, Donnie. It's time to stop drinking and start thinking." She glanced up at the Ford dealership wall clock perched on the back wall. It was a few minutes after two in the afternoon. "A little early, isn't it? And on company time, I might add."

Kash kept quiet. After all, she had a point.

"I'm sure it's five o'clock somewhere," he replied.

"What does my watch say?" She held up her wrist.

"I don't know. I can't see it from where I'm standing."

Sandra marched over and thrust her timepiece up to Donnie's face.

"It says '*now*'," Donnie said, flatly.

"And *now* is all we have. The past is history and the future is never guaranteed."

"Can't argue with that," Rev chortled.

"Get me another feature car," Sandra demanded, while prying the drink out of Donnie's hand. She pounded it back and wiped her mouth with her arm as she returned to stand beside her father.

"Did she just finish my—?" Donnie looked gobsmacked.

"Yup," Rev blurted out. "She's a chip off the old big-block alright."

Beads of sweat decorated Donnie's forehead. He locked eyes with Kash. It was time to come up with something good or walk out defeated.

"Well," she said, tapping her foot. "What ya got?"

Donnie stood tall and rubbed his neck like there was an imaginary noose hanging around it. His mind has to be racing, Kash thought, trying to come up with something brilliant. Then out of nowhere, Donnie spoke.

"Well…we'll sell Billy's race car."

"Hah! That Swiss cheese on wheels!" Cosmo chuckled. "Nobody's gonna buy that wreck."

"And in pieces," Flywheel added.

"Then put it back together and get it running."

"What about the bullet holes?" Miss Sabrina asked.

"Leave them. It gives the car character. Once it's done, we'll pitch it as 'the barn-find of the century.'" Donnie cast a wide grin like he had just cracked a 20-year cold case.

"Sounds crazy to me, but what do I know?" Cosmo said.

"No, no, he might be on to something." Kash felt a rebirth of confidence in his team. It gave him goosebumps.

"We'll need to get a jump-start on the publicity," Miss Sabrina piped in, nearly launching off her seat.

"Yes." Kash zeroed in on her. "I want ads published in every major car magazine, and issue a press release right away. When news breaks of these two features coming to auction, buyers will be lined up down the road."

"Consider it done."

"What about a venue?" Sandra asked.

The mood quickly turned somber as memories of the previous location became top of mind.

"Why not have it right here?" Soney asked as he broke the awkward silence.

The comment caught Kash off guard. "What did you say?"

"I said, have it here. We have the room for it, and we can show off our company."

"I'll be damned. What do you make of that?" Donnie asked Rev.

"Still waters run deep," Rev replied as he raised his glass to Soney, who responded with a nod.

"I think it's a great idea," Sandra said to her father. "What do you think?"

"It's simple, yet brilliant," Kash replied as he glanced at his business partner for another opinion. "Donnie."

"Saves time and it's cost-effective. I only wish I came up with the idea first."

"Great job, Soney. Keep those thoughts comin'," Kash said.

"Do we have an emcee?" Miss Sabrina asked, making notes.

"The one and only, Jacques Poirier," Kash replied.

"There's still one problem." Sandra paced the floor. "We need a segue to get buyers revved up for the big event."

"Like some sort of nostalgia sell-off?" Miss Sabrina hesitated a guess.

"What about auctioning off old gas pumps?" Cosmo suggested.

Flywheel snapped his fingers. "Or neon signs."

"Yeah, maybe even vintage mascots," Jel offered.

"No. Something that nobody else has done." Sandra clenched her fists in frustration.

Donnie grinned.

"You holding back a secret?" Kash asked.

"Automotive artwork."

The crew cast mixed emotions.

"And where, pray tell, are we going to find that?" Rev asked.

"I know just the place."

Chapter 24

On the day of the sale, the weather was clear with a gentle breeze. Since dawn, guests had been pouring in, some from around the globe. Police directed traffic from a mile away and parking overflowed the grounds making it necessary for buses to shuttle in the crowds.

News of the grand affair attracted record numbers. Some visitors embraced the gala dressed in their favorite period clothing to pay homage to the era, while others came to witness history in the making, and maybe even own a piece of it.

With the front doors pegged open, folks funneled through the main entrance, past security, and onto a velvet-roped footpath that steered them to Miss Sabrina at registration. Wearing a long red dress, hair propped ever-so-fashionably off to the side, her innocent smile gave the warmest welcome as she handed out an auction catalog and directed buyers into the restoration area. It was the precursor to the main event.

There, Kash and Donnie, outfitted in tuxedos, greeted every bidder. But as charming as they were, they could not hold the attention of guests, who drifted into the makeshift, but museum-quality showroom to an ensemble of vintage automotive art and jewelry. It was an undeniable attraction to any one person who possessed disposable wealth and an appreciation for the finer things in life.

The upper walls exhibited large, framed renderings by the artists of early automakers, including Duesenberg, Bugatti, and Rolls-Royce. The floor space was neatly organized in rows with some of the most ostentatious bling. There were old, custom-made gold rings that carried the faces of great automotive pioneers and marques, including miniature scale objects like a '37 Ford grill decorated in small diamonds.

Added security watched ogling onlookers gaze at the irreplaceable relics—from obscure car motif tie pins and bracelets to one-of-a-kind pocket watches presented under glass.

The atmosphere was electric as Jacques orchestrated the bidding from atop a small, wheeled podium affixed to a lectern. He appeared sober, but the day was still early. Dressed in 1930s plaid golf attire, complete with dual-tone spectator shoes and a Gatsby ivy cap, Jacques delivered the pedigree on a large sketch of the infamous Tin Goose— the prototype to the low production Tucker automobile—referred to as lot number 12-of-49.

Bidders hung on his every word, his fervor and passion. By the time Jacques was prepared to open the bidding, paddles were raised high in the air. "I haven't even started and you're already willing to spend your hard-earned dollars. I must say, we're off to a smashingly good start, aren't we?"

The crowd broke into laughter and applause as Donnie and Kash kept watch while they perused the room.

"The turnout is incredible!" Donnie said.

"So far, so good." Kash enjoyed the action—from the first-time bidders to the more experienced connoisseurs who jumped in towards the end to crush the competition.

"Let's be polite about this, shall we?" Jacques suggested. "The auction estimate for this piece is between fifteen and twenty-five thousand, which I feel is a bit undervalued. We'll start with five-thousand-dollar increments, and to show that I recognize good value when I see it, let's cut to the chase and begin the bidding at twenty-five thousand."

No paddles dropped from view.

"I have a bid for twenty-five thousand. Now thirty thousand. Thirty-five back in the corner. Now forty. Fifty thousand! Wow, thank you, Madame, a ten-thousand-dollar leap on that one," he said with delight. "Do I hear fifty-five thousand?" Jacques scanned the room.

A gentleman dressed as Charlie Chaplin raised his paddle, wiggled his mustache, and nodded.

"I now have fifty-five thousand from Mr. Chaplin."

A few giggles broke out from the assembly.

"Sixty thousand," voiced a woman with a Gibson Girl hairstyle, holding the arm of her husband at her side.

"I now have sixty-thousand," Jacques repeated. "Now sixty-five— no, I'm sorry, Mr. Chaplin is pointing to the ceiling so I'm going to assume seventy, correct?"

The man dressed as Chaplin smiled and nodded one more time.

"Wow, another ten-k jump. Thank you, sir."

The man obliged by tipping his bowler.

Jacques scanned the room again for additional bidders. "I now have seventy-thousand." He held the gavel in hand.

"Seventy-five," came a lady's voice from the back of the room. Dressed in a stunning hourglass Dior dress, she waved her paddle feverishly.

"Seventy-five," Jacques repeated. "Obviously our experts greatly underestimated the value of this piece. Do I hear an even eighty?"

The Chaplin character raised his hand.

"Eighty thousand!" Jacques exulted.

The audience gasped.

Jacques waited for the woman in the back row to counter as she gazed at her husband for approval. He shook his head "no."

It was time for Jacques to move on and perhaps find an individual contemplating one last final bid. "Going once at eighty thousand."

But, there were no other bids.

"Eighty thousand going twice, and…" He dropped the hammer. "Sold to Mr. Charlie Chaplin at eighty thousand. Bidder number…?" Jacques paused as the man raised his paddle. "One-zero-one. Thank you, sir."

An applause followed the sale.

Jacques was on a roll. He had the spectators captivated and the bidding wars were underway.

By ten-thirty in the morning the foretaste was over, and the volume of guests moved outside where they could enjoy the array of just over 200 memorable classics on manicured grounds surrounded by oak trees. A handful of coupes were positioned on berms to highlight the most coveted and desirable automobiles of the twentieth century while a massive tent held seating for more than a thousand patrons who waited impatiently for the show to begin.

Under the big top, a quintet of musicians played classical hits from Beethoven to Tchaikovsky, and a catering service set forth assorted meals, sweets, and beverages to quench the thirst and appetites of avid buyers.

From center stage, the first dozen collector cars were lined up in formation while a drone hovered above to capture it all on video.

The outdoor event was even more of an adrenaline rush than the morning's sale. Reporters had stormed the grounds, some anticipating a moment that might upstage the stolen Corvette from the previous auction.

In the middle of it all stood Kash with Donnie by his side. The *Bullitt* Ford Mustang and Billy's Lotus 38 were angled around them as the media scrum began.

"Do you think this is the highlight sale of the year for you?" one newspaper reporter asked.

"I believe this sale is the finest moment in our company's history," Kash said. "We'll look back and be very proud of what we've accomplished here today."

"What's the overall estimated value of automobiles onsite?" another journalist asked.

"Somewhere in the neighborhood of twenty-five million dollars."

"Whew!" came an outburst from the reporters who looked at one another, enthused with wide smiles.

"What stands out differently about this sale from your others?" a female journalist asked.

"For starters, we've beefed up security so there shouldn't be any attempts at grand theft auto," Kash joked as the media chuckled in tune. "Also, we have the highest number of top-quality classic and vintage automobiles we've ever had at auction. Our General Manager, Donnie Kars…step closer Donnie," Kash invited, as he felt a need to credit his business partner. He placed an arm over his friend's shoulder. "Donnie, along with our entire crew, have worked tirelessly to bring you the most exciting venue possible."

"There is speculation of financial troubles with Kash and Kars," the reporter added. "Care to comment?"

"Despite the rumors, our company has remained very profitable," Kash said. "We are getting bigger and better with every sale. And today is proof of that."

"What do you say to your competitors who feel your company is run by a bunch of former jailbirds?" a heavyset journalist asked, obviously looking for a headline.

Kash sighed. "Well, let me set the record straight. I grew up in a time when people believed in the American dream. Now part of that included giving deserving people a second chance in life. All of these 'former jailbirds', as you put it, including me and Donnie, have paid our dues. We don't spend much time looking in the rearview mirror these days when we know the view in front of us is all that matters."

"What can you tell us about the two feature cars?"

"I'm glad you finally asked," Kash wiped the sweat from his brow. "We've got the original '68 Ford Mustang GT from the movie *Bullitt* that's been in a private collector's hands for decades." He turned to witness Sandra sitting on cue behind the wheel of the celebrity automobile. "Fire it up."

She turned over the engine. A loud, deep rumble shot through the dual exhaust.

"If you recall, we recently sold one of the famous *Mad Max* cars for several hundred thousand dollars. Knowing these automobiles can be quite a draw, we're confident the *Bullitt* will set the highest record for any movie car at auction."

Photographers gathered around the vehicle to take pictures as Sandra punched down on the gas pedal so the V8 could roar.

The hairs stood up on the back of Kash's neck as he recognized that familiar engine sound from the film. "Makes me feel McQueen is right here with us."

Donnie waved at her to shut it down. As the engine died, applause broke out along with a few cheers by nearby spectators, who marveled at the beauty and sound of the iconic vehicle.

"What about the barn find? The Billy the Kid race car?" another reporter asked.

"That's our other great feature." Kash turned to his right and garnered a quick look at Rev who was waiting with both hands on the steering wheel.

The hood to the Lotus 38 was propped open so journalists could see the impressive engine, detailed and polished to a nickel shine.

"This was Billy the Kid's beloved race car, and it stayed untouched for decades until it was recently discovered. It's certainly one for the history books and I think it'll fetch big bucks."

Donnie nodded at Rev to turn over the engine. As it fired up, the photographers scuttled over for a closer look. The high-pitched engine revs rattled every loose panel, nut, and bolt.

"It looks pretty rough," one reporter said.

"Well, this is a partially unrestored example, with exception of course to the engine which we overhauled and brought back to its original condition."

"Is that a bullet hole?" another journalist pointed out.

"Maybe," Kash said as he looked at Donnie with chagrin. "What you're witnessing is a true tour de force. And if you want to own the Holy Grail of 1960s legendary race cars, then this is it. It's the only survivor of Billy's known to exist."

Donnie signaled Rev to shut off the engine.

"How are you going to outdo yourself on the next sale?"

Kash smiled. "I'll leave that part up to Donnie and the rest of the crew to figure out."

"Ladies and gentlemen," Jacques announced from the podium. "The auction will commence in five minutes. Please take your seats in the bidding area."

"That's our cue, ladies and gentlemen. Thank you for coming today," Kash said as the media dispersed. He turned to Donnie. "Well, what do you think?"

"Win or lose, I don't think we could have done any better."

"I agree," Kash said. "C'mon, let's go grab a seat and watch the show."

Chapter 25

A thunderous roar cut through the air as the first vehicle of the day made its debut under the big tent towards center stage. A shiny, black '53 Ford F100 with a choppy idle motored up to the auction block.

After playing a Tchaikovsky piece, the classical musicians took a break as the pickup drove past.

Kash and Donnie took a seat in a reserved section of the first row.

Jacques walked past them with a Scotch in his hand. "Someone here today is going to own that beautiful beast." He raised his glass and continued onward.

"Well it looks like Jacques has already started celebrating." Donnie glanced at his watch. It was approaching eleven o'clock in the morning. "I hope he can keep it under wraps."

"If he wants to get paid his ten grand, he better," Kash replied, scanning the room. "Have you seen any sign of Dugan?"

"Nope. Not yet." Donnie was geared up for the auction, tapping his hands on his knee while humming a tune. He peered at Kash. "Relax. You got nothing to worry about. There's security everywhere." He caught a glimpse of all the eye candy—not the cars, but the waitresses, dressed in matching Playboy bunny outfits—carousing with clients and handing out assorted hors d'oeuvres. "Excuse me," he said to one of the lovely servers walking past. "I'd like a few of those."

"Of course," she replied, handing Donnie a small plate as he selected goodies from her tray.

He offered a few samples to Kash. "Here. Take some."

"No thanks, I'm good."

"Suit yourself."

The hostess wandered over to an older, debonair-looking man dressed in 1920s formal attire when Sandra arrived and took a seat next to her father.

"Where did you find these women? At the local strip club?"

"Very funny. It just so happens they have lots of experience," Donnie replied with a mouthful.

"I'm sure they do."

"I mean at waitressing." He wiped his face with a napkin.

"That's enough, you two." Kash had bigger concerns on his mind.

"I'm telling you, these ladies are only gonna drive sales up," Donnie bolstered.

"Keep in mind we're selling an image here, today." Sandra gestured to herself as an example. She was wearing a formal black dress and looked both elegant and professional.

"Gorgeous women and beautiful cars go hand-in-hand. There isn't a hot rod shop around that doesn't have one of those chick calendars hanging up."

"He's got a point," Kash said, nonchalantly.

"You're agreeing with him."

Kash shrugged and glanced over at Donnie who was smiling and licking his fingers.

Sandra glared at her father. "Don't you see what he's up to? These women are going to pose with clients for photos. Then Donnie is going to take those images and threaten to post them online unless the client makes a purchase."

"It's worked before." Donnie nestled into his seat and stretched his legs. "It's called leveraging." He pointed at Kash. "Besides, look at them. They're doing a great job." Donnie blew a kiss to one of the servers—a Marilyn Monroe look-alike—posing with an older gentleman dressed in a Hawaiian shirt and shorts.

"Just keep it discreet," Kash instructed. "The last thing I want is our company name tied to blackmail."

"Ah, did someone say blackmail?" Dugan asked as he approached with the Mishka brothers at his side. "That would be a costly humiliation."

"Speak of the devil," Sandra said quietly to her dad as she folded her arms and crossed her legs.

Just then, Donnie's cell phone rang. "Saved by the bell," he said as he got up from his chair and moved away to answer the call.

"I was wondering when you'd show up." Kash was hoping he wouldn't turn up at all.

Dugan leaned on his cane and the rubber tip sank into the ground. "I've come to witness your last big hurrah."

"You remember my daughter, Sandra."

"How can I forget? She has the beauty of her mother."

Sandra rolled her eyes.

"And the disposition of her father." Dugan shook his head in dismay.

"I hate to tell you this, Dugan, but today we might break a record," Kash said.

"I'm sure you'll manage to break *something*," he snickered. "By the way, I see you've made Billy's race car one of the entries."

"It's actually one of the feature cars."

"Of course, we had to dig the lead out of it first," Sandra remarked sarcastically.

"Had I known you were planning on putting it in the sale, I would have shot it to pieces," Dugan scoffed as a server swung by with a tray of champagne. He'd just snatched a glass when the engine belonging to a white '66 Oldsmobile Toronado cranked over and backfired, startling the crowd. It sounded like a shotgun as it resonated across the tent.

"Here's to going out with a bang." He took a sip. "Now, if you'll excuse me, I see the gong show is about to start." He nodded at Sandra before leaving. "My dear."

"Good morning and welcome," Jacques announced upon his return to the lectern. "If you didn't attend this morning's sale, then we have not met. My name is Jacques Poirier and I will be your primary auctioneer for today."

A round of light handclapping erupted from the crowd.

"I would like to take this opportunity to introduce to you the man responsible for making this all possible. Without further ado, please give a warm welcome to the President and CEO of Kash and Kars, the one and only, Mr. Thomas Kash."

Cheers and whistles soared as Kash stood, turned to face the audience, and waved. He was then surprised by a standing ovation. Flattered, he nodded at Jacques before returning to his seat. As the guests settled down and made themselves comfortable, Jacques opened the bidding on the first vehicle of the day.

For the next few hours, it was a non-stop sell-off of one automobile after another, some setting never-before-seen high prices. Despite two temporary setbacks, a classic that failed to start and a flat tire, the sale was moving along splendidly.

As the sun reached its peak, Jacques called a brief intermission. Donnie rushed to the stage to fill in, but before he could get to the mic, the musicians started to play a tribute to Led Zeppelin that got people to kick back and groove to the music.

At about the same time, ringman Gordy King, who had been working buyers steadily since that morning, approached Kash. "You better come quick. There's a problem."

Without a word, Kash darted towards the lineup of cars. There, he saw the '68 *Bullitt* Mustang getting shoved off to the side. Soney and Cosmo were pushing from the back bumper as Rev steered.

"What's going on?" Kash asked as he approached the driver's side.

"The car's out of the auction," Rev snapped.

"Says who?"

"The owner. He even took the keys right out of the ignition."

"Why?"

"He wouldn't say."

Kash looked around for the seller, only to spot Dugan watching closely from the sidelines. Fighting back his outrage, Kash confronted him as the orchestra ramped down for Jacques to enter the stage and introduce a '76 Triumph TR-6.

"I suspect this is your doing?"

"I'm just a spectator," Dugan replied.

"Really. Why else would the *Bullitt* be pulled?"

"Maybe the seller got cold feet."

"Or maybe you were determined not to see it sell." Kash wanted to grab hold of Dugan, but the Mishka brothers were standing guard. "Do you know where I can find him?"

"Perhaps tied up in the trunk," Dugan said with a crooked smile as he crossed his arms. "What are you going to do now, Kash? You're out one feature car, and that leaves you with that wreck you call a barn find. I'd say it's starting to look a lot less in your favor."

Kash wasted no time arguing. Instead, he headed off to return to the iconic movie car, where he discovered Donnie.

"What the hell's going on?"

"Your feature's out. I believe Dugan somehow got to him and scared him off."

"For Christ's sake, we need the *Bullitt* on the block in less than an hour!"

"Just panic slowly. We'll find the owner and sort this out. We can't rightfully sell the car without him feeling assured."

"The hell we can't! We have a signed contract. If he doesn't let us auction it, we'll sue."

"By the time we do that, Dugan will have taken over this company."

"So, what do you propose we do?"

"I want you to try and pin down the owner. In the meantime, I'll have Jacques delay the sale of the Mustang."

Donnie grabbed his cell. He dialed and waited for it to ring while looking over at Kash. "We need to unload this car if we're going to survive."

"We still have Billy's race car, don't forget."

"I think you'll be lucky to get what you paid for it." Donnie raised a finger as he paused to listen. "Ah, it goes straight to voicemail."

"Well, keep calling and get security to help you search the place. He's bound to show up at some point."

As the two departed, Kash approached the stage, waited for Jacques to drop the hammer on the sale of the TR-6, then waved him over as the next automobile was being driven up for viewing.

"We're having some issues with the *Bullitt* so skip over it for now," Kash instructed.

The smell of Scotch rolled off Jacques's tongue. "Sounds rather skive, mate."

"I'll keep you posted."

"Righto." Jacques appeared a bit tipsy as he returned to the lectern.

Kash sensed the crowd becoming impatient as he was approached by several high-end buyers asking when the features would hit the block. "When the timing's right," he responded cordially before moving on.

While the 149th car of the day had just found a new owner, Donnie brought forth more bad news.

"I can't find the owner of the *Bullitt*," he said, looking deflated.

"Alright." Kash nodded. "You know what to do next."

Donnie instructed the cocktail waitresses to double up on the free champagne to every potential bidder in the house. He then asked for the servers to take time to pose with potential buyers in a 'very friendly manner.' With the camaraderie at an all-time high, Kash signaled Jacques to introduce the Lotus 38 as the next car to hit the block.

"Folks, the moment you've all been waiting for, the historic and former Indy race car, once driven by the legendary Billy the Kid, will be making its debut on stage right here in just one minute."

Heads turned as the high-pitched sound of the Lotus caught the attention of every potential buyer under the tent. Bidders rose to their feet to take pictures and video of the momentous occasion as Rev idled the roadster towards the front. He was loaded with vintage accessories, wearing an old pair of racing goggles and a brown leather cap, with a light summer scarf wrapped around his neck. Some folks chuckled and pointed good-naturedly as he passed by with exhaust fumes pumping out the back.

Jacques sat his Scotch on the lectern as the race car stopped front and center. He strolled around the vehicle, checking all angles to establish selling points. In short, there were none, other than the fact it was driven by the legend—Billy the Kid.

A fury of conversation ignited as it parked, some speculating that the car's value would be close to one million dollars. The catalog listed its worth as "not available" as it was the only surviving documented race car of Billy's ever to reach market.

For the first time, Kash was nervous. He took a seat next to Sandra, grabbed her hand, and held it firmly, then whispered a prayer asking Billy for a miracle.

On one side of the stage, several large historic photographs planted on easels featured the late Billy the Kid, including one image of Kash standing alongside his mentor. On the other side stood a collage of images depicting the motorcar soaring around the Indy track just moments before Billy's untimely death.

By now, Kash was a little choked up and fought back tears as his daughter comforted him by nestling into his side.

"It's the bee's knees," Jacques announced with delight. "The only Billy the Kid race car in existence!" He wasted no time with the bidding, starting at half a million, and it took off in all directions—from the floor, the internet, and phone—in a frenzy.

Increments were set at fifty thousand dollars and Jacques could not spit out the bids fast enough.

Gordy and Donnie canvassed the floor for any contemplating bidders, but it seemed there were no second-guessers. The offers flowed effortlessly.

"And I have a bid of one million dollars!" Jacques exclaimed as sweat trickled down the side of his face.

And the bids continued, hitting one-and-a-half-million, then two million, and then...

"Two-point-five million!" Jacques shouted out. He touched his cool glass of Scotch to his forehead.

It was down to three heavy hitters in the crowd, financially wrestling one another for the win.

"I can't believe my eyes," Kash muttered to himself. He could pay Dugan his money and still have funds left over to continue his business. It was a growing sigh of relief with every paddle raised.

As the value climbed to three million, only two bidders were left. Each had a motivational coach in their corner, Gordy at one end, Donnie at the other, both working each potential buyer to their maximum.

Gordy had a high-strung investment broker from New York City; Donnie, a cattle rancher from Omaha. At one point it looked like a screaming match between the two peers as Donnie and Gordy whacked the bidding back and forth like a tennis match while Jacques left the stage for a minute to get himself a refill. It was a bit of comic relief, given the intensity of the battle, which continued for about two minutes.

When Jacques returned, Donnie's buyer was the top bidder at three point two million.

At the opposite side of the room, Gordy hammered away at the investor, who kept quiet, stroking his silvery hair.

Jacques gently tapped the gavel and interrupted. "Gordy, how much further is your client willing to go?"

"All the way," he hollered back, but the investor shook his head that he was out.

"If you come up just a bit more, I think you'd own this lovely, one-of-a-kind, race car." It was as if Jacques was giving his own pep talk. "Let me ask you something. Please stand up for a minute."

The broker stood and straightened his Armani suit.

"Have you ever seen a Brinks truck at a funeral?" Jacques asked.

Laughter broke out from the audience.

"No, I'm serious." He repeated the question.

The broker shook his head.

"And why is that?"

There was a bit of a lull, then Jacques spoke.

"Because you can't take your fortune with you when you die. So, if you really like the bloody car, then don't let the money stop you from buying it."

The man nodded in agreement and the bid was raised another fifty thousand.

After a couple more bids it finally came to an end, and Jacques dropped the hammer at three point six million dollars, selling the car to a very gratified cattle farmer who anxiously made his way to the front to momentarily trade places with Rev behind the wheel.

Dugan was furious and almost snapped his cane in half attempting to get up and leave with his henchmen.

Making his way to the podium was Kash. "Congratulations, sir." He led with a firm handshake.

"Thank you," the cattleman replied. "Would you kindly autograph the dash for me?"

"But I'm not Billy the Kid."

"No, but you were the closest thing to him."

Kash, hearing those words, nearly wept as he pulled a Sharpie from his pocket and honored the request. The two posed for photos next to the new purchase. A television journalist covering the event pulled the buyer aside for a brief interview as Kash wandered over to thank Jacques for his efforts.

As the Lotus crossed the block, only to be replaced by yet another vehicle to sell, Kash returned to his seat.

Sandra rewarded her father with a heartfelt hug.

Donnie joined in and wiped his tears away. "We did it!" he said. "We're in the clear for once and for all."

"I never thought I'd see the day." Kash was never happier.

Sandra gazed at her father with admiration. "I knew you could pull it off, dad."

"It was Donnie's idea to sell Billy's car. Not mine."

"I mean all of this," she said.

"I only wish Billy were here to see how much he's still adored."

"I'm sure he is."

Kash sighed heavily, as if a great weight was lifted off him. "I'm gonna step outside and get a breath of fresh air." He nodded at Donnie to follow.

"Alright. I'll see you both back here in a few minutes," Sandra replied.

Outside the tent, Rev was waiting in the Lotus. "I'm gonna park her in the corral. Do one of you want to come for a ride?"

"No thanks," Kash said as he rested against a pink, rocket-finned '59 Cadillac Eldorado Biarritz.

"I'll pass," Donnie replied. "Love the outfit by the way."

"Thanks," he said with an actual smile, before pulling away merrily.

As Jacques could be heard announcing the next vehicle on the block, Donnie pulled out two Cuban cigars from inside his jacket. "I was saving these, just in case." He handed one over to Kash, then revealed a Zippo.

"Doesn't that belong to Soney?"

"Possession's nine-tenths of the law," he chortled.

The two lit up and relished in a few puffs before exhaling the smoke.

"I would have liked to have seen the expression on Dugan's face when the hammer dropped." Donnie exhaled a perfect smoke ring.

"I saw it, and it felt great." Kash took another drag.

"About time he gets a taste of sweet revenge."

A blonde server winked at Kash as she approached with a tray of drinks.

"I think I'll have one of those." He reached for a glass.

"Good idea." Donnie followed suit.

As she left, Kash made a toast. "To better days ahead."

"Amen to that."

A shot echoed in the distance as Donnie took a swig. Something hit the swooping rear fender of the '59 Caddy. It made a loud metallic noise, enough to startle Kash.

"What the hell was that?"

Donnie kept himself occupied, enjoying the aroma of his Cohiba. "Sounded like a fender bender."

Kash examined a hole that had ripped through the sculptured sheet metal, peeling it back like a banana. He scanned the back of the property along the tree line as a small waft of smoke emerged from a bush when a second round whizzed by. A sunken feeling washed over him as he turned to face Donnie who had an expanding bloom of red branching out across his chest. "Dear God!"

Donnie trembled. His mouth gaped open, his cigar nosedived to the ground, and his drink slipped from his fingers, landing haphazardly on the manicured lawn. He fell to one knee before keeling over as Kash rushed to his side.

"Get down! There's a shooter," Kash yelled at a handful of guests strolling by, when a third shot cut through the air. It struck another section of the Caddy's rear end.

Screams rang out as folks ducked for cover.

"Better days, huh?" Donnie choked on his words.

"I need help over here!" Kash shouted. "Somebody call 911!"

Donnie turned pale and began to shiver.

"Don't close your eyes. Stay focused," Kash demanded as he watched his friend's breathing become shallow and weak. "Just hang in there."

Laying on the soft grass among the serenity of the beautiful marques, Donnie drifted into unconsciousness.

Chapter 26

A few days later…

Jel pulled up to the curb outside the Toska restaurant in his '69 Chrysler 300. It was a little before eight o'clock in the evening and the streets lay empty for a Tuesday night. The old movie theater across the street had the odd customer strolling through its front doors.

Stretching his arm out across the top of the seat, Jel stared back at his passenger. "You sure you don't want me to come with you?"

Wearing his fedora, bomber jacket, and jeans, Kash sat in the middle of the back seat with a duffle bag stuffed with money at his side.

"Nah, it's best I handle this on my own."

Jel reached into the glove box and pulled out a .357 Magnum. "At least take this, you might need it."

"No thanks," Kash said. "Just keep the engine running. If I'm not back in fifteen, hightail it outta here." He exited the car and jogged up the steps to the tavern with the bag in hand. Once through the doors, he was greeted by the host.

"Good evening, sir. Welcome back."

Kash nodded at the gentleman and moved past him to scan the room. Dim lighting made it a bit challenging, but there was Dugan sitting at his usual back table, consuming his expensive wine and chewing his meal like a king, as his goons stood close by.

Upon approach, Kash tossed the bag onto an empty chair nearby, snagging the linen and knocking over an empty wine glass. "Here's your final payment."

Looking unimpressed, Dugan continued cutting into his rare steak. "You should remove your hat in a restaurant. It's not polite." He dabbed his lips with a white napkin.

From behind, Jonah reached to remove Kash's fedora, when he received an unexpected closed fist to the groin. The big man dropped to the floor, crying out in pain. His twin brother Abe rushed forward to intervene, but Dugan was quick to react.

"That's enough!" he shouted, pounding a fist on the table. "Abe, help your brother up and take the money into the kitchen. And count it twice. I want to make sure it's all there."

Jonah got to one knee, staring up at Kash. He looked ready for revenge as Abe helped him get to his feet.

"Don't even think about it," Kash said.

Dugan chuckled. "Ah, still got some fire in the belly." He leaned back into his seat as a waiter swung by with a steaming bowl of seafood consommé. "At least prison prepared you for something." He crossed his arms to make himself look comfortable. "Now, if you don't mind, I'd like to eat my shark fin soup while it's still hot."

Kash grabbed the bottle of Domaine Leroy Richebourg Grand Cru, 1949, and took a swig.

Dugan was not impressed. "Next time, use a glass."

Kash backwashed in it.

"You just ruined a six-thousand-dollar bottle of wine, you uncultured swine!" Dugan exclaimed.

Kash banged the bottle down and reached across the table to pull Dugan up by his collar. "You listen to me, you gutless coward."

Dugan looked around, desperately searching for the Mishka brothers.

"I swear I'll finish you right here before you can signal for help."

"God damn you," Dugan hissed as he struggled to break free.

As a second waiter appeared out of nowhere, Kash released his hold and Dugan fell back into his seat with a thud.

"Everything alright, gentlemen?"

"Fine," Kash replied, thinking the server was a ruffian with his scarred face and slicked back hair.

"Can I get you anything?"

"Yes, another bottle of the same." Dugan straightened his shirt and tie. "This one's been ruined."

"Right away, sir." The waiter removed the bottle and left on his mission.

"Donnie's lying in a coma, clinging to life, because you tried to gun him down!" Kash aimed a finger at Dugan.

"I'd be very careful throwing around false allegations." Dugan swirled a piece of steak in its marinade.

"Well, who else would try to kill Donnie?"

"Maybe you should speak to the fella who tried to steal your beloved Corvette." Dugan took a bite.

The waiter returned, wine in hand, and offered to pour. Dugan slid his glass across the linen.

"Chevelle," Kash said with doubt. "But he's in jail."

"Actually, he made bail a few days ago." Dugan raised his glass for a toast. "Gotta love the legal system." Setting the glass under his nose, he sniffed the aroma, then took a sip. "Perfect."

The waiter nodded and quickly disappeared.

"Where is he?"

"I have no idea, but I'd be *very* careful with him."

"Why's that?"

"He's the best of the worst kind of people. No conscience. No remorse. Kinda' admire him, actually."

"How do you know?"

"'Cause I know all the bad guys." Dugan grinned, showing off his lack of dental hygiene.

It was a lot to digest as Kash ran his fingers through his hair. "How bad is he?"

"Makes me look like a pillar of the community." He tasted his soup. "Needs a little pepper." Dugan fumbled around for the shaker. "Take it from me. You best arm yourself."

Abe stepped out of the kitchen. "Money's all there."

Dugan nodded and waved him off. "Well Kash, consider your debt paid in full."

Kash grabbed the wine glass laying on its side, poured himself a celebratory drink, then held the tumbler up to a small overhead chandelier to see if he could spot something special about the costly wine. He couldn't. "I'll find Chevelle on my own."

"You still have his car?" Dugan took another spoonful.

"Yeah."

"Then he'll find you." He stabbed his fork into another piece of meat and swished it around his plate. "And that won't be too difficult."

"I'll see ya, Dugan." Kash rested his drink and turned to leave.

"Au revoir."

Strolling out of the restaurant, Kash felt relief when he saw the 300 still by the curb. He swung open the rear door and jumped into the back seat.

"Well," Jel said. "How'd it go?"

Kash locked eyes with him. "I might need your gun after all."

Chapter 27

I nside the restoration area, Jel was installing a new set of spark plug wires on Destiny, when Rev tapped him on the arm.

"Hey Jalopy. Boss wants you in his office, pronto." Grease was smeared across Rev's face and coveralls.

"Oh, what for?"

"He didn't say, but come back right away so we can get this damn thing finished. We got a schedule to keep."

Rev traded places under the hood with Jel while he rushed across the floor, pushed open the double doors leading to the hallway, and entered the office.

Kash sat behind his desk loading bullets into the chamber of the Magnum. On the desk sat his cell phone, keys, and a few scattered papers.

"You wanted to see me?"

"Yeah." Kash flipped the barrel closed and put the gun in a drawer when the desk phone rang. "Just hang on a second." He picked up the receiver. "Kash here." A pause. "Uh-huh. Yeah. I'll be right there." Kash hung up and jumped to his feet, then reached for his jacket and fedora from a hall tree. "That was Sandra. She's at the hospital." He threw on his bomber and snatched his keys. "Donnie's up and talking."

"That's great news."

"I'm gonna need to rush out, but I wanted to ask you, how's Rev treating you?" Kash straightened his hat.

"Okay. He apologized to me and Soney."

"Good."

"But he still calls me Jalopy."

Kash chuckled. "Consider it a compliment. I think he's finally warming up to you." He fluffed his collar.

"I guess I've been called worse."

"If it's any consolation, you do make one heck of an addition to the team."

"Thanks."

"I'll see you soon." Kash fled out the door.

For the first time since leaving prison, Jel felt a sense of belonging. As he turned to leave, he noticed Kash's cell phone still sitting on the desk, grabbed it, and ran back to the shop.

Rev was still under the hood of Destiny when Jel approached him.

"Did Kash come through here?"

"Yeah, like greased lightning. Headed straight out that door." Rev pointed with a screwdriver.

"He forgot his phone." Jel put the cell in his shirt pocket and plopped himself into the driver's seat.

Rev rested a hand on the frame of the windshield. "What's going on, Jalopy?" He shot Jel an inquiring eye.

"Donnie's out of his coma."

"Thank God." He sighed in relief.

"And Kash is on his way to the hospital to visit him right now."

"Well, on that note, let's add to the celebration by starting this thing up. Get ready to crank her over." He poured a few ounces of fuel down the twin carburetors from a plastic cup that had been resting on a tool cart.

As Rev stepped back, Jel reached for the keys and spun the engine. The mighty V8 turned a few times without a spark.

"Keep pumping the pedal and try it again," Rev instructed.

On the next attempt, the engine burst to life with a fierce groan. The sound caught everyone's attention. Cosmo flipped up his welding shield and shut off his torch. Soney stopped buffing the tailfin on a '59 Caddy, and Flywheel holstered his soldering gun.

A flame shot back out through the top of the carbs, followed by a stall. It was apparent that the engine was starving for fuel.

"Hang on a second," Rev said as he poured another few ounces down the carbs.

Out of the corner of his eye, Jel spotted a man in the rearview wandering through the large bay door. He resembled an outlaw biker, dressed in boots, jeans, and a black vest. A thin, chrome chain was clipped to a belt buckle. His face was unshaven and his black hair was tied back in a ponytail. "Looks like we got a customer."

"That ain't no customer," Rev warned as he recognized Chevelle, who was heading straight towards them. He grabbed a tire iron from the tool cart.

Jel took his fingers off the ignition and waited to see what would happen next.

"What the hell do you want?" Rev asked.

Chevelle smirked, his lit cigarette wedged in the corner of his lips. He removed his dark shades to admire the Corvette's makeover up close. "Wow. She looks better than when I first laid eyes on her." He exhaled a line of smoke, which floated over the roadster.

"Put your mitts on that car, and I'll crack your melon wide open!" Rev pointed the pry bar at him.

"Easy, old-timer." Chevelle raised his hands as if to calm the situation.

"You've got some nerve showing your face around here!" Rev grumbled, crossing his arms.

"I've only come for my wheels."

"You'll have to talk to the boss and he ain't here."

Chevelle stepped forward and Rev raised his arm to strike.

"You really gonna take a swing at me, Reverend?"

Rev nodded. "Nothing would give me more satisfaction."

"You're supposed to be a man of God." He moved closer to Rev.

"I am, and you're about to feel his wrath right upside your head."

"You ain't got it in ya," Chevelle said, toying with him.

"The hell I don't." Rev wound up as if to hit a home run.

Jel jumped out of the car and stepped between Chevelle and Rev. He was jacked like he could bench press any car in the place, his denim shirt appearing painted over his chiseled upper body.

"Whoa." Chevelle treaded backward to assess the enormity of his adversary. "You're even bigger than that damn Indian." He paused to look him over. "But I bet you ain't bulletproof." He reached inside his jacket like he was going to withdraw a pistol.

"You best think carefully about your next move, 'cause I might just put whatever it is you got hiding in that jacket where the sun doesn't shine."

It was an uncommon tone coming from the gentle giant, but Jel had dealt with Chevelle's kind before.

"I guess I'll come back another time," he snickered.

"Maybe you should book an appointment, like everybody else," Rev replied.

"Mind if I use the restroom before I go?"

Jel pointed to a weathered door in the corner of the garage that led to a toilet and sink. Chevelle wandered over and pulled the door shut behind him as the staff resumed their work.

"Should have told him to tie a knot in it," Rev commented as he put down the pry bar. "Be sure to escort him out of here."

A minute later, Chevelle strolled out of the washroom and pulled up his zipper. He left the same way he entered, but with Jel tagging behind.

Out back in the lot sat a Harley-Davidson Fat Boy resting on its kickstand, accompanied by a cute, leggy blonde dressed in leathers.

Chevelle turned to Jel before mounting the bike. "Tell your boss he better have my wheels ready or else it's gonna get ugly." He revved the throttle as the blonde hopped on the back.

The woman ogled the big guy like she was in the market for a new boy-toy. "What's *your* name?"

Jel thought about it for a second. "Jalopy."

Chevelle glared at his female companion.

"I'm sure I'll see you around." The blonde winked goodbye as she wrapped her arms around Chevelle before the two sped off.

Shaking his head in wonderment, Jel returned inside where he discovered the rest of his peers taking a break, chatting around the roadster.

"Is he gone?" Rev asked as Jel joined the group.

"Yeah, he hit the road."

Cosmo stood, arms folded across his belly. "Rev was just saying that Donnie's come around."

"That's right."

"I wonder if we can visit him after hours." Flywheel said.

"I suggest we wait till the boss gets back and gives us an update," Rev stated. "On another note, I believe today's Miss Sabrina's birthday."

Cosmo and Flywheel smiled widely. A celebration typically meant a serving of homemade treats.

"Let's go sing her a tune," Jel urged.

"I never pegged you for a vocalist." Cosmo rubbed his jaw.

"I've sang gospel in the choir since I was five."

"That settles it then. C'mon." Rev slapped his hands together and led the team into the front office where Miss Sabrina had just hung up the phone.

The men broke into a lovely serenade, singing *Happy Birthday*. Jel and Soney had great baritone voices, while Rev sang opera-style with a hand placed over his heart. Cosmo did his best despite his face shield repeatedly falling closed, muffling his vocals, while Flywheel struggled to find the harmony.

As they reached the end of the song, Miss Sabrina stood and applauded. "That was really wonderful! Please, have some!" She pointed to a plate of homemade tarts and pastries.

The men attacked the desserts like animals.

"These are incredible." Jel grabbed a second mini lemon meringue pie, and then another.

"Reminds me of my mother's baking." Cosmo removed his face shield so he could cram a butter tart into his mouth, while Soney followed suit.

"C'mon, back to work, boys. We still got another hour to go." Rev licked his fingers, then grabbed the last dessert before leaving.

As Jel threw open the double doors to the shop, the crew was horrified to witness flames engulfing the restroom.

"Fire!" Rev yelled, running for a nearby extinguisher as smoke billowed through the bay doors.

Cosmo hollered at Miss Sabrina to call 911 while Flywheel scrambled to reach a small hose connected to a water tap. He cranked open the valve and ran off to douse the flames.

The blaze had conquered the wall adjoining the bathroom and was headed towards the trusses. Despite Rev attacking it with the extinguisher, it was obvious that it would be soon out of control.

It was déjà vu for Jel, who had experienced the same eerie feeling when his speed shop went up in smoke. Snapping back into the present crisis, he hustled to save the vintage Corvette. At first, the car didn't want to start. "C'mon," Jel shouted while pumping the gas pedal. As the engine sparked to life, he jammed the shifter into reverse and backed out into the parking lot.

Returning in full stride, Jel dashed behind the wheel of the '59 Caddy, but the keys were not in it. He shifted the gear selector into neutral and got out to push, using all his might to roll the beast outside.

By now, sparks that would eventually engulf the entire structure were fanning across the overhead beams, igniting little splinters of dry wood.

Rev had tossed the depleted extinguisher aside when Miss Sabrina came running in, screaming.

"Oh my God!" She was frantic, jumping up and down, her hands pressed against her face.

"This is no time for hysteria!" Rev shouted. "Get those flammables outta here."

Soney pitched in, and grabbed two heavy fuel cans while Miss Sabrina gathered up all the oil containers. One by one, she hauled them outdoors.

Flywheel continued to spray water, but there wasn't enough pressure to reach the ceiling. It was only a matter of minutes before the crew would be overwhelmed.

As a fire truck pulled into the lot, sirens blaring, there came a flicker of hope. A handful of firefighters, prepared for battle, jumped off the vehicle as it slowed to a halt.

The crew ran out of the building as the captain stepped forward to lead his team. "Is everybody out?"

"Yes, we're all accounted for," Jel replied, coughing from the smoke.

"Good," he replied as his team opened valves on the truck to douse the flames. In short order, the fire brigade headed in to tackle the blaze.

Twenty minutes later, the frenzy was over, but the damage to the structure was extensive. Two firemen were still pouring water on the charred wood frame when Kash showed up to witness the aftermath.

His crew ran over to him. Miss Sabrina couldn't stop crying as gobs of mascara continued to run down her face. The rest of the team was blackened with smoke and grit—a sign that they had all fought hard to try and save the building.

"Is anyone hurt?" Kash asked, pale from the discovery.

"We're okay." Rev coughed as he wiped his mouth.

"I forgot my cell and came back to get it." He appeared shell-shocked at the sight of his torched business.

"I have it," Jel said as he handed it over.

Cosmo tried to soften the blow. "It's not as bad as it looks." He spat on the ground, then wiped his grimy face with his hand.

"What happened?"

"We don't know," Flywheel replied, wiping away the dirt from his clothing. "We went to the front office to wish Miss Sabrina a happy birthday, and when we got back the place was ablaze."

The captain of the fire team approached the crew. "Which one of you is the owner?"

Soney let out a discreet cough and pointed to his boss.

"I am," Kash replied.

"I'm afraid the building is unsafe for anyone to return to for a while."

Just then, a section from above collapsed onto the hydraulic lift where the '61 Vette had sat only a short while ago.

"I see your point," Kash said, staring at the disaster.

"Hopefully you can salvage something outta there eventually." The captain moved on, waving to his staff to finish up as they surrounded the area in yellow caution tape.

"Chevelle's to blame for this," Rev said.

"Yeah, he must've tossed his cig in the bathroom garbage," Jel added.

"Wait a minute. Chevelle was here?" Kash asked, surprised.

"He showed up just minutes after you left." Jel rubbed one of his sore shoulders, having strained it to move the Caddy. "He came for his wheels."

"Does this mean we're out of business?" Flywheel asked, looking concerned.

"Yes, what are we going to do now?" Miss Sabrina wiped away her tears.

Kash examined the carnage. Sections of rooftop smoldered in ruins on the floor, and at the end of the building where the fire had started, the entire wall had become ashes. In the middle of it all sat the only recognizable item left standing—the toilet—an island surrounded by debris. Looking back at his team's melancholy faces, he spoke. "There's only one thing *to* do."

"What's that?" Jel asked, thinking it was the end of a promising future.

Kash was tight-faced and serious for a few seconds. Then a glimmer of hope appeared in his eyes, followed by a confident grin. "We start over," he said with the utmost assurance.

About the Author

KASH and KARS is the debut novel from Steven J. Repergel. A published freelance writer since 2001, he is an honors graduate from the University of Windsor where he majored in communications and film studies.

Inspired by the teachings of his mentor, Dr. Wayne Dyer, Repergel reignited his passion for storytelling nearly two decades ago with a series of written automotive articles that were published and distributed internationally. A classic car aficionado and fan of iconic automotive-themed movies, such as *Mad Max* and *Bullitt*, Repergel first played with the idea of *Kash and Kars* as a screenplay. After careful consideration, and driven by his love for writing, he decided to develop the story into a novel.

In addition to writing, Repergel works as a professional communications consultant, and resides with his family in the rural community of Welland, Ontario, Canada.

www.KashandKars.com